D0284122

Black Crossing

By

C. K. Crigger

Print Edition
© Copyright 2016 C.K. Crigger

Wolfpack Publishing

P.O. Box 620427
Las Vegas, NV 89162

ISBN: 978-1-62918-517-0

Chapter 1

October, 1887

A CORPSE SWINGING in the wind greeted TJ Osgood as he stepped from the stagecoach onto Black Crossing's main street. Briefly uncertain as to whether his eyes were playing tricks on him, he peered through drenching rain as thunder rolled overhead. A second glance confirmed the first. Sure enough, that was a man dangling at the end of a rope. Spinning and twisting, with his neck forced into an unlikely angle by the knot beneath his left ear.

The apparent liveliness of the victim was not caused by any present struggle against his fate. Blame instead the northerly wind blowing out of Canada and the hanging tree's swaying branches. Any fool could see the man was dead, and Osgood was no fool. More, he had a bit of experience in matters like these. It appeared to him the body had been there a while.

He shivered a little under the wind's blast. The grisly presence of the dead man was less than welcoming to anyone considering Black Crossing, Idaho as a new home. Osgood had hired on as marshal of this rough little town, and it looked like the place might prove a tad more interesting than he'd been led to believe.

He sighed. Could be he was too worn-out to take on complicated matters. Could be he was getting too old.

Shorty, the driver of the Spokane-Wallace Stage Lines coach, tossed Osgood's two valises down into his arms, apparently without noticing the new marshal's weariness. "Here you go, Marshal Osgood," he said. "Delivered safe, sound, and on time. Glad I'm just passing through today. Don't envy you staying on and trying to keep these folks in order, that's for sure."

"A little unruly, are they?" Osgood's gaze was fixed on the gallows.

"Some ain't so unruly as they used to be, looks like."

Osgood noticed Shorty avoided looking at the hanging tree's gruesome fruit. The driver hadn't even gotten down to stretch his legs, although he must've been stiff as broom straw. Instead, he kept the lines in his hands and watched the horse's ears twitch as he waited for the postmaster to bring out the mail. Odd he hadn't gone into the stage office looking for hot coffee, or something stronger, to counteract the chill rain that had pelted down throughout the morning. He acted as if he could hardly wait to get out of town.

Osgood blinked against a renewed downpour as the sky opened up again, and jerked his thumb at the body. "Who is that feller? Do you know him?"

"No, sir. I sure don't. What's more, I don't care to hear about him, either."

And that, too, in Osgood's opinion, was strange kettle of fish. Stage drivers were usually better than a newspaper, the way they spread word of doings in a territory.

The postmaster trundled outside into the rain with a slim bundle wrapped in a portfolio of greased buckskin. "This is all the mail today, Shorty," he said, passing it up to the stage driver. "Better get it over to Wallace before the road floods out. Got a couple of important documents in there. Mr. O'Doud asked for special delivery. "

Shorty tucked the packet under the seat, out of the wet. "Do my best, Will." He touched his hat. "Marshal, best of luck to you."

Osgood nodded, aware of the sharp glance the postmaster slanted towards him. The crackers on Shorty's whip popped over the six-horse team with a sound like exploding fireworks. Dodging clods of mud that flew from under the horses' hooves as they lunged into the harness and sped off, Osgood limped forward, his hand outstretched.

"Pleasure to meet you, Mr. Dunfolk," he said.

Dunfolk's hand moved forward reluctantly, as if he distrusted the touch of the new marshal's palm. "Likewise," he said, in a tone implying his reply was open to discussion. "How'd you know who I am?"

The question sounded almost suspicious. Osgood pointed to the sign above a door leading into the dark interior of the building that was both stage stop and post office. "That says the postmaster is Will Dunfolk. I heard the stage driver call you Will, and took you for the postmaster. Am I mistaken?"

"Reckon not. And I suppose you're Black Crossing's new marshal. The former Pinkerton detective Colin O'Doud hired for himself from outta San Francisco. Heard about you. Heard you'd been shot."

Heard? Osgood wondered sourly. Or read off the postcard he'd sent O'Doud when he accepted the job. "You're partway right," he said, struck by how bitter Dunfolk's comment sounded.

"Huh?"

"I said, you're only partway right. I am Marshal TJ Osgood, and I was shot. But it's my understanding the town of Black Crossing is paying my wages. I work for the town, not any one man." He couldn't make it any plainer than that.

Dunfolk harrumphed. "You'll find O'Doud's signature on your pay stub every month, mister. He owns this town."

Osgood eyed the stubby postmaster. "He own you?"

"No!" Dunfolk sputtered. "Not me. No."d

Maybe he protested too much.

"Well then," Osgood said, calm and reasonable like, "I expect someone has to sign the pay voucher. All part of the mayor's job." He moved until he stood beneath the eaves overhanging the storefront. In the distance, thunder rumbled again. "Who is that feller?" he asked, nodding towards the gallows. "What did he do to earn himself a rope necktie?"

Dunfolk's silence avoided the question, but Osgood outwaited him. At last, the postmaster shrugged. "He was one of our local boys. Seems he had too big a mouth on him. He's been hanging there since court got out yesterday afternoon. For the rest…guess you'd better ask O'Doud."

"Since yesterday?" A bad taste filled Osgood's mouth. "Why hasn't the body been taken down?"

"Ask O'Doud," Dunfolk said again. "Or Jensen, his…foreman."

Osgood could tell Dunfolk wasn't going to say more. "I see," he said slowly, not really seeing or understanding anything at all. "Well, sir, I'll do that. Now, if you'll show me where the marshal's office is, I'll be out of your hair."

The postmaster didn't seem to be the most forthcoming conversationalist in town, Osgood observed. Looked as if he, or anybody else here, wouldn't so much as sniff, unless it was on the mayor's say so.

Dunfolk was pointing across the road and eastward, indicating a raw-wood building sitting by itself in the center of the next block. Iron bars covered the one window that looked

4

onto the street. A trace of smoke, almost invisible through the downpour, blew from a stovepipe sticking out of the cedar-shingled roof. At least somebody was keeping the place warm.

Osgood was aware of Dunfolk watching as he slogged through the mud toward the office. There were other folks examining him, too. He felt the probing of their eyes. But not a one came forward either to welcome him or to curse him. Strange. As strange as a man left hanging by the neck in the middle of town.

There wasn't much to Black Crossing, Idaho Territory, he found. Mostly just a wide spot on a trail cut through the timber that sat on the banks of a stream. It was a logging town, which meant it had evolved out of the forest. Aside from the one main street as the core, a few other businesses and some dozen or so houses and cabins meandered up the hillside, scattered amongst the last of the standing timber. The town struck Osgood as being dark and closed-in, with the forest too tall and thick for his taste. He wondered if the sun ever broke through. Didn't feel like it, cold as it was.

His boots were heavy with clotted mud before he swung open the door of the marshal's office. Heat blasted him in the face. Blessed warmth that reached out and touched his aching knees and sore leg. The odor of wet dog and wet wool, burned leather and scorched coffee permeated the room. There was a man sitting on a kitchen chair less than a foot away from the stove, his stocking feet propped on the wood-box. Apparently he'd been napping. When Osgood slammed the door shut, the man jumped to his feet. A nondescript dog, part hound, part something else, raised its head.

"Coffee's boiling over," Osgood said. It was hissing onto the stovetop, dancing in beads.

"Yipes." The man reached barehanded for the handle, jerked the pot onto a cooler part of the stove and stood, shaking his fingers. "Thanks, mister. Don't want to burn the pot dry."

Osgood sat his valises down by the desk and eyed the young feller standing in front of him. O'Doud's letter hadn't mentioned a deputy, but unless his middle-aged eyes were failing him, the lad had a tin star pinned to his shirt. He hardly looked old enough to apply for a job, although his size was substantial. A roll of baby fat hung around his belly. His face, plump and rosy, with wide cheekbones, bore a faintly Slavic cast. His eyes were a vibrant blue.

"What can I do for you, mister?" The deputy grew more flushed under Osgood's careful scrutiny.

"I'm TJ Osgood. You've heard of me?"

The deputy's mouth firmed, drew downward. "Yes, sir. You're the new marshal." The words were not particularly warm.

Osgood glanced out the barred window, whose view was mostly of the gallows' burden. Raindrops sprayed from his hat onto the rough wood floor as he beat it against his thigh before setting the Stetson back on top his head. "Would you care to explain to me what that's all about?" No wonder the deputy had had his back turned to the window.

The deputy refused to follow the direction of Osgood's gaze. "Explain, sir?"

"About that body out there, Deputy…"

"Tompko, sir. My name is Benny Tompko." He thrust out a large, thick hand and gave Osgood's a perfunctory pump.

"Well, Deputy Tompko, I reckon you'd best put on your coat and hat and come with me." TJ flexed his fingers, somewhat surprised to find his bones uncrushed. With strength like that, the best idea was to put the deputy to work.

Benny appeared more than eager for some kind of action. "Yes, sir. I'll get my shoes. Is there trouble?"

"I hope not."

Tompko's steaming socks, drying too close to the stove, had been the source of the wet wool odor. He wrestled them on, then pushed his damp feet into high-topped brogans. "Where we going, Marshal?" he asked, reaching for the coat hanging on a peg.

"We're going to cut that body down, Tompko, and outlaw or no, see he gets decently planted."

The deputy, in the act of anchoring his hat under his chin, paused. "We are? That's fine by me, sir, but there's folks here apt to quibble. I was told to keep Isaac up there until Sunday morning. Said Isaac should serve as an example to any other timber jumper thinking about moving in on O'Doud territory."

"Timber jumper?"

"Yeah. They said Isaac was cutting logs on Mr. O'Doud's property."

An edge to the lad's intonation sent a little frizzle scooting along Osgood's nerves. "And was he?"

"I don't know," Benny said. "Don't know why he would've been." He turned a face full of misery toward Osgood. "Whole deal don't make any sense to me. Isaac wasn't no thief!"

"Tompko…" Remembering the postmaster's cool reception, and the stage driver's rush to get out of town, Osgood gave a care to what he wanted to say. "This Isaac kid, he did have a trial, didn't he?"

Benny squirmed as though he was uncomfortable in his body. "I…I…yeah. First trial I ever seen. Had old Judge Pringle presiding."

"Judge Pringle, you say. Not Judge Doerner from Coeur d'Alene City? Met him myself, this A.M. Seemed a competent man."

"No, sir. It was Judge Pringle. Although—"

Osgood interrupted. "But there was a jury?"

"Yes, sir." Benny's answer dragged out of him.

That much was a relief. Osgood decided to ignore the hesitancy he heard.

"Leaving the body out there—whose idea is that?"

The deputy, overwhelmed, let his head sink onto his chest. "I can't remember. But it don't seem decent to me, even if—" He stopped, as if he'd said too much.

Osgood shook his head. "A decision like that is outside the public's authority, deputy. From what I've heard, a body displayed in warning went out of fashion some years back. Anyhow, I run this office now. I'm...we're... paid to uphold the laws and keep order in this town. You do what's right, boy, and we'll get along fine. We're taking the body down."

A smile wide as a jack 'o lantern's grin split Tompko's face. "Yes, sir," he said, holding the door open for Osgood to go first. "There's some folks ain't going to like it, though."

It sounded to Osgood like the deputy took satisfaction in that.

The street remained empty of all but blustery wind, driving rain, and one bedraggled horse tied in front of the saloon with his rump turned to the storm. Outside the marshal's office, Osgood and his deputy climbed the steep steps—a series of stacked boxes—to the gallows platform. The platform itself was a makeshift affair of empty beer kegs and raw wood planks situated directly beneath the branches of the big Ponderosa pine. The dog, having followed them outdoors, cocked a leg and whined as he sprinkled the base of the tree.

Osgood heard Benny whispering under his breath, although the wind carried the words away. He thought maybe the words were a prayer. There was no doubt in the world a bit of divine help was needed here. The dead man hung with his extended neck twisted to one side, like a broken doll. His face was empty, his eyes turning milky, his skin as gray as ashes.

The end of the rope had been pulled taut, wrapped around a brace and knotted tight. Too tight, being wet and nearly frozen, for Osgood to loosen with his fingers.

"I need some slack. Grab him by the waist and lift him up," he told Tompko, taking the skinning knife he'd been meaning to hone from his boot sheath. "I'm going to cut the rope."

"Yes, sir." Tompko hesitated only fractionally before complying with Osgood's instructions.

The body was stiff, the rigor mortis, having been retarded by the chill weather, not yet passed off. Even so, Osgood

8

smelled the stink of decay already setting in. He held his breath as he sliced at the rope above the looped noose. There was a tear leaking from the corner of Tompko's eye, he noticed, as the deputy took the cadaver's full weight in his arms.

"You know this lad pretty well?" For a lad it was. Maybe only sixteen or seventeen years old and slightly built. Made it hard to believe he was a desperado in need of hanging. The deputy was not much older.

Mutely, Deputy Benny Tompko nodded. "His full name is—was Isaac Gilpatrick," he said, finding his voice. "And mister, his ma is mad as hell at the men who done this."

Chapter 2

TJ OSGOOD HAD NOTHING against women. He had, in fact, cared more than he wanted to admit for one or two. But the truth was, when taking his line of work into account, he'd grown to hate the sound of the word, mother. Dread welled up in his mind. "This kid had a ma?"

"Well, sure. Ain't ever body?" Tompko asked.

Osgood's mouth opened and closed. His deputy had a point. But he'd learned by now the worst part of a job like this was dealing with mothers, whether it was one who denied her boy had gone bad, or one he had to tell her boy was dead. Although this time he expected the responsibility wasn't his, on principle he purely hated the thought of getting between any woman and her son.

"Not quite what I was getting at, deputy," he said, grunting as the stiff rope fibers began to part. "My fault. I didn't expect to find a claim jumper to be a local lad is all, with family in the same territory where he's doing his stealing."

"Not a claim jumper," Benny corrected. "Timber. Or so they say."

Osgood couldn't see much difference.

"Besides which," Benny added, "he didn't do it. I know he didn't. Somebody lied."

A final whack of Osgood's knife sliced the rope in two, releasing the body into the deputy's arms. From the water-green cast of Tompko's complexion, Osgood thought he'd best not waste time taking up his share of the burden.

"Somebody? Who? Why? Hold him," he said, descending platform steps made slimy by the unrelenting rain as fast as he could. His leg, still only half-healed from the wound he'd taken six weeks ago, protested against bearing his full weight until he was safely on the ground. "All right. Lower him down."

Benny grunted with the effort of lifting the body over the side of the gallows without dropping it in the road. "I ain't mentioning anybody's name where they can hear," he said, "but I know who wanted him out of the way."

"Who?" Osgood asked, but the deputy, concentrating on his wholly repugnant business, didn't reply. Osgood thought he could answer his own question anyway.

The dog crouched beside the platform, moaning as the dead boy's legs dropped in front of his nose. "Shut up," Osgood told the dog. He grabbed the body and held it upright.

"Is there an undertaker in town?" he inquired, as soon as Tompko landed beside him. "I expect the boy's ma will want him laid out proper."

"Yeah." Benny looked more sorrowful than ever. "Undertaker's over behind the store. Mr. O'Doud owns it."

"The store or the undertaker's parlor? I thought O'Doud was a logger." And the mayor, he reminded himself. The man who will sign my paycheck.

Benny took hold of Isaac's feet, hooking one in each hand. "He is. But he owns both of them other buildings, too. Rents them out. I dunno if Mr. Ritter will do Isaac up for a funeral, Marshal. Mr. O'Doud—"

Osgood interrupted. "Let me worry about that. You just lead the way, deputy."

"Yes, sir." With no further argument, Benny led off. Osgood carried his share of the burden, gripping the corpse's shoulders as they crossed the street and eventually ducked through a narrow alley between the mercantile and a rooming house. "Short cut," Benny said.

Osgood thought they must be a sight to behold. A regular parade, what with two men carrying a bottom-heavy body folded between them, while a whining brown dog followed behind. The only missing ingredient was an audience. Nary a soul poked a head out into the rain to watch, as far as he could tell. And that was another curious thing.

Tompko stopped in front of a small, windowless shed. "This is it." Unwilling to let go of Isaac Gilpatrick's legs, Tompko kicked at the shed door with one of his heavy brogans. Then they waited, cold and uncomfortable, while rain oozed between neck and coat collars.

"Where is everybody, Tompko?" Osgood asked. "Only town I've ever seen this quiet in early afternoon was a ghost town."

"This here hanging has folks upset, Marshal. Upset and scared."

Ah. An object lesson. Osgood supposed in that light, a purpose had been served. This town would tolerate no stealing within its jurisdiction. At least, he hoped that was the lesson to be learned. And yet, the situation struck him as mighty peculiar. Other places, the hanging of a criminal was likely to be cause for a celebration, not this shuttered silence.

"Kick that door again, Deputy. Someone is in there stirring around. I can hear him."

Benny complied, nearly breaking through the bottom one-by-eight plank in his zeal, but the door remained closed.

A flare of temper lit inside Osgood. "I wish you'd tell me plain out what's going on in Black Crossing, Tompko. No more skipping around the subject."

Benny shifted uneasily, Isaac's corpse bobbing between them. "Don't know as I'm the one you ought to be asking, Marshal."

"You're my deputy, aren't you? Who else would I ask? So far, the only other Black Crossing resident I've spoken to is Dunfolk, and he said less than you."

"Ain't nobody wants to rub Mr. O'Doud's fur in the wrong direction. Might wind up like poor old Isaac here."

Benny was whispering into the turned-up collar of his coat by then, and Osgood had to guess at the deputy's last few words. Scowling, the marshal twisted around until he could give the door a couple of wallops with his own foot, exclaiming as pain radiated from the still-raw wound.

"This is the marshal," he called, his voice rough. "Open up in there before I arrest you."

A voice quavered in answer, although the words were belligerent. "What would you arrest me for?"

"Obstructing justice," Osgood said.

The feller on the other side of the wall must have believed him, for the door creaked open. It was dark inside the shed, with barely enough light to see a man-sized, stout wooden table situated in the center of the room. Osgood pushed past a wizened little man, Benny perforce following, and laid his half of their burden on the table. Freed of the weight, he found his arms and shoulders trembling from the unaccustomed strain. The bullet he'd taken in his leg must've robbed more of his strength than he'd realized. Even so, his relief was not so heartfelt as Benny's sigh.

"You're the new marshal, eh? I'm Ritter." The undertaker hadn't stirred from the doorway. "Heard you was comin'. All-fired convenient of you not to get here yesterday, wasn't it?"

"Beg pardon?"

"Never mind." Ritter allowed the door to swing shut, pitching them all into absolute darkness, but he had the layout well memorized for presently a match flared and was held over the wick of a tin kerosene lantern. With that lit and the wick adjusted, he and Osgood settled back to survey one another.

"Where'd O'Doud find you?" The undertaker spoke first.

"I came up from…" Osgood broke off the explanation, and forgot the part about him working for the town, not for O'Doud. It hadn't had much effect on Dunfolk. Somehow, he didn't suppose it would on Ritter either. "I understand this kid, Isaac Gilpatrick, lived with his family hereabouts. His ma…anybody know if she's been told what's happened? I expect she'll want to take care of the burying."

Ritter shrugged. "How should I know if Miz Gilpatrick's been told? Ain't that the business of your office?"

"Ordinarily, I suppose. Or the county sheriff's." Osgood looked at his deputy. "Benny?"

Tompko swallowed like he had a lump in his throat. "Yeah. Dunno if I was supposed to, but I walked out yesterday—afterward—and told her. Worst thing I've ever had to do in my life. She took it real hard, Marshal. Doesn't know what to do, now he's gone. She's mad enough to chew down a tree with her teeth. Talking kind of wild."

This was twice Tompko had mentioned Isaac's mother being angry. "Don't you mean she's sad?" Osgood asked, frowning.

"Well, yeah. That, too." Benny's mouth twisted. "Guess she'll have to plant Isaac with the money she's been saving. What she wanted was to send him away to school. Isaac was real smart, Marshal. He was going to study on being a doctor."

Ritter spat on the dirt floor. "Guess he wasn't smart enough to stay out of some folks' way. Is there gonna be trouble over this, Marshal? Over cuttin' the kid down early, I mean. I don't want the mayor or his men blamin' me for bringin' him here. That foreman of his can be pure snarly if he's crossed."

"Anyone has a problem with it, you send them over to me. I'll either be at the office or around town somewhere," Osgood said. "Meantime, find a box to put the boy in, and bill the county for your trouble. If Mrs. Gilpatrick wants a better casket and a service, she can pay over and above the county's share."

"Bill the county?" Ritter's mouth worked and he spat again. "O'Doud ain't gonna like that neither. He won't sign off on it."

"He'll sign," Osgood said. "This was a legal execution, wasn't it? That makes it a county obligation."

It wasn't until he and Deputy Benny Tompko were returning to the marshal's office that he noticed he'd somehow fallen into the trap of identifying the mayor as the town.

Back in the office, their sodden coats dripping from pegs and wet boots set near the stove to dry, Benny and Osgood padded across the rough floor, snagging their socks on splinters. The dog hogged the prime spot in front of the stove, steam rising from his soaked fur. Osgood shivered. For the first time in months, the desire for a shot of whiskey hummed through his mind. With an effort, he shrugged the thought away.

"Gummer it, Badger, move!" Benny tripped over the outstretched dog, slopping a dab of water out of the bucket as he refilled the coffee pot. Without opening its eyes, the dog let out a wide yawn, but didn't budge. Benny stepped over him.

"That his name—Badger?"

Benny flushed. "Well, that's what I'm calling him. He don't answer to it very well, though."

"Is he your dog?"

"Naw…well, yeah. Maybe." Benny couldn't seem to make up his mind one way or the other, whether he wanted to claim the mutt. "He just wandered in. I give him a soup bone now and again. Marshal Blodgett never minded him being around."

"Speaking of Marshal Blodgett…" Osgood opened a door set in the wall behind his desk, one he'd barely noticed on his earlier, lightning fast inspection of the marshal's office. He figured to find the way out to the privy. Instead, he found a short hallway with two more doors, one of which was made of thick pine planks. A three-by-twelve inch window was set in the upper quadrant of the door that, for now, stood open on a narrow cell. Inside the cell were a couple of double-tiered bunks—a folded blanket on the bare mattresses—an empty water bucket and a slop bucket, also empty. An odor of old vomit and older urine eddied into the hall, where another door led outside. "Didn't know there was a holding cell," he said.

"Come Saturday night, it's always full."

"Speaking of Marshal Blodgett," Osgood resumed, turning to Tompko once more. "Why did he leave?"

Tompko, in the act of dipping a scoop of ground coffee into the pot, froze. "Well, he didn't exactly leave," he said, keeping his back turned to Osgood.

"Quit?"

"No. Not that either. Old Marshal Blodgett wasn't no quitter."

Osgood eased the cellblock door shut and clipped the latch. "Benny, I think you're trying to make a point. Come right out with it. What happened to him?"

"Well, he died, kind of unexpected like."

Osgood waited, but Benny, his concentration on settling the lid on the coffee pot, didn't volunteer any particulars.

"What did he die of, Benny?" Osgood asked. He had a cold feeling it hadn't been old age.

When the young deputy looked up, his eyes were weepy again. "He was shot. Shot in the back. Bushwhacked just outside of town. He'd taken a prisoner up to Wallace that day, looking to see if the feller's boss would pay his fine and get him off our hands. He never made it back."

"Murder," Osgood said slowly, the cold setting up camp for a long stay. "Did you catch who did it?"

Tompko's chin firmed. "Some tried to put the blame on Isaac for that, too, but his ma wouldn't stand for it. She wasn't even here then, but she telegraphed to Coeur d'Alene City for Sheriff Farnsworth. He come over and poked around, but turned out he couldn't pin it on anybody, for sure. There just wasn't nobody a feller could point his finger at, but he did clear Isaac."

"How long ago was this?"

"Couple of months. The middle of August."

Osgood supposed the advertisement for an experienced lawman must have gone out right after, because he'd been hired on September 3rd. And then, his last day on the San Francisco job, he'd been shot in the leg when he got caught in the middle of a bank robbery. Any trail Blodgett's murderer might've left behind was long gone by now.

Benny poured them each a cup of scalding coffee. He was setting Osgood's in front of him on the desk when the office door banged open, bounced once and scraped across a high spot in the floor. Benny jumped, sloshing coffee onto the desk and the marshal's hand. Badger sat up on his hind end and growled, lips curling back over his fangs.

"Come in and shut the door," Osgood told the newcomer. "No sense heating the whole outdoors."

The man who entered was trouble, he suspected. Trouble with a capital T. His open, rain-soaked duster was pulled back, displaying double holsters with the gun butts facing front. The holsters were tied-down for ease in drawing his weapons. From his outward appearance, he struck Osgood as neither a typical logger or miner, nor yet a businessman. Gunslinger, or hired assassin suited his look better.

The man's intense, almost colorless eyes bored into Osgood's. Without so much as an aye, yes, or no, he said, "On whose authority did you cut that timber-jumping young hooligan down? He was supposed to remain on the gallows until Sunday. Mr. O'Doud isn't going to like this." His voice cracked like a whip.

"Benny," Osgood said, his narrowed gaze never breaking contact with his uninvited guest. "I'll trouble you to hand me that smaller valise, if you please." Only when the valise was open in front of him did he look away. Stored inside the bag was a well-oiled gun belt and a .44 Smith & Wesson revolver with worn walnut grips. He took the pistol from the holster and laid it in front of him on the desk.

He looked up. "You were saying?"

"Don't play with me, Marshal. If you are the marshal. I don't see the badge."

Osgood reached in the valise again, found the brass, five-point star he'd received earlier today at his swearing in, and placed it beside the.44. "TJ Osgood, sir. Duly confirmed this morning by Judge Edwin Doerner in Coeur d'Alene City. I never play when it comes to either business or the law. Who are you?"

The man waved this aside. He had fine hands, Osgood noted. Well cared for, with slender fingers and tender palms. The mark of a gunman or a gambler. Judging by the arsenal he wore, Osgood opted for the first.

"Tell him who I am, kid." The gunman addressed Benny, who was surreptitiously mopping up spilled coffee with his shirtsleeve.

"This here is Mr. Jensen. He's Mr. O'Doud's...uh..."

Osgood waited for Benny to finish—a wait that grew overlong. "Mr. O'Doud's what, Benny? Suppose you fill me in on what it is you do, Mr. Jensen." He winked at Benny.

Jensen flushed. Osgood thought it came from anger, not embarrassment.

"Mr. O'Doud won't like what you did, Osgood." He cut his sharp stare towards Deputy Benny Tompko. "The kid here should've told you about Mr. O'Doud's instructions. Didn't he?"

"He told me." Osgood sipped coffee, burning his tongue.

"Then what the—"

Osgood, his voice quiet, overrode Jensen's outburst before it got fairly started. "I couldn't go along with the idea," he said. "Goes against mandated application of due process." He wasn't sure about the mandated part, but it sounded right to him. "So I cut the boy down. Took the body over to the undertaker where it belongs, 'til it's claimed by next of kin. That's only decent. Now, Mr. Jensen, is there anything else?"

Jensen's thin lips worked. "Mr. O'Doud wants to see you. Said for you to come out to his house for supper tomorrow night. Six o'clock—sharp." He flung himself around in a whirl of coattails and stepped back out into the rain.

It almost seemed Benny had ceased to breathe until Osgood said, "Shut the door, Benny, and throw another block of wood on the fire. Mr. Jensen seems to have let in the cold."

Benny shook himself, toeing the door closed. "What're you going to do, Marshal?"

"Do? About what?"

Benny gestured. "Him. O'Doud." He bent to the wood box, selected a chunk of wood and, after opening the front of the stove, tossed it in.

"Guess I'll go eat supper with the mayor tomorrow night, for one thing. But first, I'd better see about getting myself a room. Is there a hotel in town, Benny? Or better yet, a boarding house?"

"Oh, you've got your own cabin, Marshal. Right out back. Comes with the job."

A warm hotel room sounded more inviting. One with a dining room where there was a good meal available for the asking. Find a little company and conversation. Osgood could imagine entering a cabin that had stood empty for two months. Empty, except for creeping varmints and maybe the memories of a murdered man. He shuddered—a goose walking over his grave—and wondered if he was sickening of something again.

Stomping his feet into boots slimy with damp, Osgood stood up and buckled the gun belt around his lean waist. Not bad for a forty-year-old man, he reflected, using the last hole punched in the belt. But he couldn't claim all the credit. Some of his present thinness came from the infection and subsequent fever caused by the wound in his leg.

In view of these last two hours, he had to wonder if he was ready for a lawman's job. He guessed there was more here than met the eye, and none of it pretty.

"How about you showing me this cabin, Deputy. I don't suppose it comes supplied with a housekeeper and cook."

Tompko didn't so much as crack a smile at the weak joke. "No, sir. But there's a café over on the other side of the post office. It's my ma's place. She'll see you get a good supper."

"I'd be grateful, Benny."

Tompko led them out the back, through the wind-driven rain and along a narrow, pine needle strewn path until they reached a log cabin no larger than the front room of most San Francisco houses.

"It ain't much," Benny warned, digging a key from a space between logs and forcing it into the big, old-fashioned padlock securing the door. "But it don't cost you nothing either."

Osgood pushed into the cabin behind the deputy. The waning afternoon light allowed him to locate a coal-oil lamp sitting on the mantel above the native stone fireplace. He went over and lit it, replacing the glass shield.

"Stinks in here," Benny said, looking around.

"Smells like mice and mildew. Cold, too." Exactly as he'd envisioned.

"There's wood." Benny pointed to a full wood box. "I'll start a fire for you, Marshal."

"Thanks." Osgood set his valises on the bare rope springs of the bed. He'd need to buy a few things tomorrow at the mercantile. Set up housekeeping for himself. There was a trunk coming on the next freight wagon, but he hadn't thought to bring a mattress.

Snorting, he put aside thoughts of his comfort and turned to what worried him most. "I asked before, Deputy, and reckon I'm still not clear on the answer. So, I'm asking again. Did Isaac Gilpatrick have a fair trial, with lawyers and witnesses and a jury of his peers?"

Tompko gulped. "Oh, he had a trial, all right. Don't think there was anything fair about it. And I guess I don't know what 'peers' is, but I can tell you he was caught, tried and executed all in one afternoon."

Osgood's innards twisted. "Who caught him, Benny? Who arrested and charged him? Not you, I know. Was it the sheriff?"

"No, sir. Sure wasn't. Bunch of Mr. O'Doud's yahoos said they caught him cutting timber out on O'Doud's stumpage. They worked him over, then trussed him up and brought him in to town."

"Proof?"

"His word against theirs. And there was more of them."

"But there was a judge at his trial?"

"Yeah, there was a judge. I told you. Old Judge Pringle that Mr. O'Doud rushed down out of Wallace yesterday morning. They had him ready before they even took Isaac prisoner. I think the judge was deaf, 'cause he sure wouldn't listen to what Isaac or any the rest of us tried to say. Just O'Doud's men."

"And this jury, they said Isaac was guilty?"

"Yes." The word hissed out of Benny. "They were all O'Doud's men. Same ones that beat him up and brought him in. But..."

"And the judge sentenced him to hang, right then and there?"

"He sure did." The tears were back in Benny's eyes.

Osgood's innards churned. "Where'd they get a hangman on that short order?"

"One of the witnesses volunteered."

"And the order that the body was to swing from the gallows for twenty-four hours—that come from this Judge Pringle, too?" Osgood asked. "Did the sheriff agree?"

Gallows! What was he talking about? They'd been in such a rush they'd hanged the boy from a tree limb. Judge or no judge, what he was hearing sounded like a lynching, not a properly conducted execution in punishment for a capital crime.

"Sheriff never got here," Benny said.

Then it was a lynching for certain. Osgood realized Benny hadn't answered the second part of his question, which probably didn't make much difference. He figured he already knew what the boy would say. "Deputy? On whose authority was the body left up? Judge Pringle give that order?"

Slowly, Benny said, "No, sir. Reckon that came directly from Mr. O'Doud. And then I had to break the news to Isaac's ma." He hiccupped once, just remembering the meeting.

***

A STAB OF FEAR had knifed through her heart when Ione Gilpatrick saw Benny trudging up the trail to the cabin. He was alone, and that right there was enough to sound a warning—the second warning.

The first was when Isaac hadn't come home from work yesterday. Anxiety had been building inside her all day. She'd tried to convince herself he'd worked late last night and decided to stay over at the logging camp. Or alternately, he'd been with Benny Tompko, helping clean up the jail before the new marshal arrived. He might even have stopped to see the girl he was sweet on, his opinion of her father not changing his regard for her.

Isaac was used to being on his own, without the need to consider anyone else. She'd only been here a week, and she still felt like his guest, not family, not his mother. He didn't need her advice anymore.

But here was Benny, his steps lagging, and when he came near enough, she saw his face was strained and set. He looked much older than seventeen, his fresh-faced youth buried in care.

Ione went to meet him with her heart thundering in her ears. They met on the front stoop. There was a chill in the air, dark clouds obscured the sky and she shivered with dread.

"Benny," she said, her voice a harsh croak.

His shoulders hunched. He forgot to remove his hat in her presence, and she was certain he'd been taught otherwise. "Ma'am," he said.

He'd been watching his feet, but when he looked up finally, she saw his mouth was trembling. Her own firmed. They were silent.

At last, when she could bear the tension no longer, she said, "Is it Isaac? Has there been an accident?"

She'd hated that he worked in the woods. There was no job more dangerous.

"Isaac's…" Benny hesitated, then blurted, "Isaac is dead."

Her chest squeezed down so hard she could barely draw a breath. "When? What happened?" She brought up her hands to cover her mouth, holding in the pain, wanting to scream a denial.

"They…they…" Benny's face twisted.

"They?"

"They brought him in and set up a court. Bunch of men testified, and the judge said he was guilty. They strung him up on that big pine tree in town."

"Guilty?" she repeated. "Isaac? Guilty of what?"

At first Ione couldn't make sense of what Benny said. He'd rushed his words, she told herself. Mumbled. She hadn't understood.

But she had.

"They?" she asked again, her voice hard. She didn't really need Benny to name names. She knew who they were. Hadn't Isaac told her, over and over? And hadn't she begged him, over and over, to drop his quest and come back home with her where he'd be safe.

He wouldn't. Timber jumping was one thing; Marshal Blodgett's murder the last straw. Isaac refused to rest until

Blodgett's murderer was brought to justice. Her fault, perhaps. Too much of her stubbornness bred into him.

And now he'd paid, but so would they. Kill her son and get away with it? No. She'd see they got what was coming to them if it was the last thing she ever did.

"Tell me everything," she demanded, and under her stony-eyed stare, Benny Tompko did.

Chapter 3

OSGOOD, LOATHE TO GO OUT in the rain again, was tempted to forego his supper. Would have, if it hadn't been for the hole in his gut reminding him he hadn't eaten since breakfast. Maybe that was why he felt so cold. Could have been his blood was thin, too, he excused himself. It was still summer in California.

Alternatively, it might've been because he was getting a real sorry picture of this town.

The fire Benny had lit in the square cast-iron stove was slowly taking the chill from the one-room cabin, although it had the unfortunate effect of making the stench worse. Osgood inspected his new home, trying not to be obvious about his dislike, while thinking Benny had told him nothing less than the truth. The place wasn't much. There was a dribble of rain leaking into northeast corner by the washstand where the roof had sunk lower than the rest. He'd have to remember to get out there and fix it tomorrow, weather permitting.

Osgood sneezed twice, forcing the smell of burning dust and mouse droppings out of his nose.

"Yipes," Benny said. "Sorry, Marshal. I should've thought to come over and open the door. Get some air in here. Maybe sweep it out a bit."

Osgood figured it would take more than an open door or a broom to clear the cabin. Water and some strong lye soap wouldn't come amiss. Tomorrow, he promised himself. "That's all right, Benny," he said. "It'll give me something to do in the morning."

He'd go over to the mercantile, purchase supplies, and while he was out spending money, he'd be shopping for something more—a handle on the character of the town. Meet people and get to know them a little. From what he'd seen so far, the prevailing attitude was one of distrust—if not downright fear. Distrust of him might be understandable, since he was new here, but he sensed folks out-and-out feared Colin O'Doud, the leading citizen.

After Benny had gone off to eat supper, Osgood allowed himself to wonder how much of his deputy's take on this situation he could rely on. Tompko admitted to being friends with the deceased. But the postmaster had echoed Tompko's attitude toward the timber baron, if a smidgeon less loudly. Ritter, the undertaker, did as well.

Osgood puttered, changing his wet socks for dry ones, although what good that would do if he was just going to tromp off in the rain again, he couldn't say. He washed his face and hands, and at the last minute before leaving the cabin, unbuckled the holster with the.44 and hung it on a nail driven into the wall by the bed. Residents of Black Crossing might be more inclined to open up if they didn't feel threatened.

Meanwhile, he judged it best not to advertise the fact he was a little spooked by today's events. Therefore, opening the smaller of his valises, he drew out his Remington Police pistol with the three-inch barrel, snugged it into the small of his back and drew his jacket down over the top. He might not want to show he was loaded for bear, but he wasn't stupid enough to go unarmed either.

When Osgood stepped from the alley beside the marshal's office, he found a few folks out on the street, braving the steady downpour to go about their business. Due to the removal of Gilpatrick's body? he wondered. Word must have gotten around because a man or two nodded a greeting as they met, and Osgood sensed approval. He tipped his hat to a woman wearing a soggy bonnet and who was all wrapped in a heavy shawl.

Steamy warmth and the delectable aroma of hot grease, yeast bread, and apple pie with cinnamon surrounded him as he entered the café Benny had pointed out. It was early, the supper rush not yet begun, and Osgood had his choice of tables. He chose a small one draped in a blue-checkered cloth that put him close to the window where he could look out on the street and yet not, himself, be seen. Years in the business of detective work and law enforcement had made him cautious.

A tall, rosy-cheeked blonde weighing a scant ten pounds more than strictly necessary appeared beside his table like a genie popped out of a bottle—or was that a lamp? Her apron, worn over the top of a tan-colored dress, matched the tablecloth.

Osgood studied her a moment. "Benny sent me," he said. "I'm TJ Osgood."

"Yah?" She tossed her head as though shaking back a mane of free-flowing hair, although she wore her blonde locks in a heavy braid. "You must be the new marshal then, I betcha. I'm Benny's ma. He iss sending more work for me, yah?"

"Afraid so. But you can't be Benny's ma. Sure you aren't his sister?"

In his experience, he'd found it never hurts to sweet-talk a good-looking woman, although in this case, the observation was true. The woman hardly looked of an age to have a son as old as Benny. And her old-world accent was quaint and pretty, too. His smile, when it came, was warm.

She smiled in return, accepting the flattery as her due.

Osgood fancied he saw a little interest that reciprocated his own. Maybe, seeing she had a son working as a deputy, she wasn't put off by what another woman had once told him was a hard, uncompromising expression. And maybe the white hair he'd recently noticed sprouting in his brown sideburns, or the crinkles beside his dark eyes, didn't bother her like it would a younger woman.

"That wass a good ting you did today, Marshal." Magda Tompko leaned nearer, speaking with a quiet voice. "Made my Benny proud, being part of it. He says you tell him a man must do what iss right. He wass friends with the Gilpatrick boy, you know. We never saw no mean in that lad."

Osgood could've told her a feller didn't need to be mean to be a thief, but all he said was, "Glad you approve." Changing the subject, he sniffed the air much as he fancied old Badger on the trail of a soup bone might have done. "Something sure smells good. What's to eat tonight, Mrs. Tompko? Stew?"

Magda slapped the air with a large, capable hand. "Stew? For you, Mr. Osgood, dere's fried chicken. Unless your heart iss set on stew."

"Fried chicken would be fine, ma'am." As though in agreement, his stomach rumbled as noisily as a freight train taking a mountain grade. His face turned red.

Magda smiled. "I be right back with your supper. Coffee?"

"Coffee sounds good."

The café filled up as he ate. Besides half a fried chicken, he plowed his way through a mound of mashed spuds smothered in peppery cream gravy, a side order of canned green beans and three fresh-baked bread rolls. The repast ended with the best apple pie he'd ever eaten, warm from the oven and spiced with plenty of cinnamon. Turned out Benny's ma baked for the restaurant, aside from waiting tables. She was almost too busy for the compliment he paid her, but not too busy for a whispered word of warning as he proffered money to pay his bill.

"Benny tell me that Mr. Jensen come to see you, Marshal," she said. "You watch him. He iss evil man. A bought man. He tink Benny is nobody and leaves him alone, but you, Mr. Osgood, you are somebody."

"Thank you, Mrs. Tompko. I'll keep my eye on him." His grin twisted. "But lawmen are natural born targets. I'm used to it."

"Magda," she said, a wide smile lighting her face. "My name. It iss Magda."

Taking pleasure from the sense of well-being, Osgood realized she was flirting with him in an easy, comfortable sort of way. He enjoyed it even more considering the other diners, for the most part, avoided his eyes as he limped past them to the door. Guilt? he wondered. Or fear?

On his way to the cabin, Osgood stopped in at the marshal's office where he let the dog out—then right back in—banked the fire in the stove and locked up for the night. Folks knew where to find him if he were needed, which, from the silence he'd met with so far, he didn't expect anyone would. It always took time to build respect and confidence when a lawman came to a new town. This one might take longer than usual, considering the circumstances of his hiring. Well, he was sorry for that, but he doubted he could change the prevailing attitude overnight.

The path from the office to his cabin was darker than the bottom of a mile-deep mine. Osgood stumbled over uneven footing—tree roots and slippery pine needles—calling himself a fool for having neglected to leave a lamp burning. The cabin was bad enough without the smothering blackness. Slowed by the sticking door, which was swollen by rain, when at last it opened, he was propelled forcefully into the room, his sore leg coming in harsh contact with the corner of the table.

"Ouch!" That didn't seem enough. "Gummer it," he added, borrowing his deputy's exclamation when his questing hands were slow to find the coal oil lamp he'd left ready. But then, with a clatter, his fingertips touched the lamp's brass base and found the wooden lucifers he'd put near. Scratching one across the rough tabletop, he set flame to wick before replacing the glass chimney.

That's when he felt movement behind him. He whirled, snatching beneath his coat for the pocket pistol, but already knowing he was too late. His eyes, dilated from looking into the lamp's heart, saw nothing more than a black blur catching at the edge of his vision. The attack he expected failed to materialize.

"No need to jump, Marshal," a low voice whispered. "I'm no danger to you."

"Who is that? What do you want?"

The light didn't reach far enough. He couldn't make out much more than that the figure was small and female.

"Come over here where I can see you," Osgood demanded.

The figure didn't move. "I don't want anyone looking in the window and seeing you have a visitor, Marshal. You stay where you are, I'll stay where I am, and we'll both do all right."

Osgood hesitated only a moment. His visitor was clad all in black, right down to the shawl draped over her hair. It shielded her face so she blended with the dark cabin walls. Her husky voice had thrown him for a minute, but now he had her pegged. Her voice was husky because she'd been crying, and he knew of at least one woman who might have cause to weep.

Almost certainly, this was Isaac Gilpatrick's ma. He'd been halfway expecting her. Changing his mind about drawing the hideout pistol, he shoved it firmly behind his belt again. He bent to the lamp and turned the wick up a notch.

"What can I do for you, Mrs. Gilpatrick?" he asked, when he faced her again.

This drew a breath of surprise from her. "How did you know who I am?"

"Easy guess. I thought you might stop by, although, ma'am, I got to say tomorrow morning would be a better time to come. How'd you get in here? I nearly shot you."

"I couldn't come in daylight," the woman said without addressing how she'd gotten in.

Osgood was grateful she refrained from pointing out that if she'd been a bushwhacker, he would've been dead before he ever knew she was there.

"Why couldn't you come in daylight?" he asked.

"Because O'Doud or his hired gun might see me. I don't want them to know who I am."

Osgood thought maybe his brains were scrambled. "You mean they don't?"

"No. I've never been in Black Crossing before."

Osgood supposed there was a reason for her secrecy, but didn't know as he wanted to go into it right now.

"That's right," he said. "I remember Tompko mentioning you're new here, too. But I don't think you need to worry, ma'am. I doubt anybody who saw you tonight would recognize you tomorrow. I'm only five feet from you, and I can't tell what you look like behind that shawl."

"That's fine," she said, making no effort to remedy his perceptions. Keeping a distance beyond the lamp's glow, she took a seat on the edge of the bed frame. "As for the rest, it's a long story, but I've only been in this territory a short while. About the only person I've met face-to-face in Black Crossing is the young man who works for you, Benny Tompko."

Osgood must have shown his puzzlement because she added, "The boys, my Isaac and Benny, were friendly, much of an age. They just sort of drew together, the way young folks do. My son came to Idaho last year with his uncle, Sean Gilpatrick, you see. Sean had been looking out for Isaac after my husband died, while I was teaching in a girl's school. But then Sean decided mining paid better than logging, and he moved on into the Coeur d'Alene Mining District.

"Isaac had met a girl and wouldn't leave Black Crossing. I didn't want my son on his own—he's only seventeen, Marshal—and there'd already been trouble. Since my job had petered out, I came to be with him. I got here just a week ago and found he was being investigated for a second time in connection with Marshal Blodgett's murder. Well, I hired a lawyer and he put a stop to that, I can tell you. But, as you can see, the persecution went on. "

Alarm spread through Osgood. He'd guessed the dead kid's age pretty close. Seventeen. Too young to die on a gallows.

Seating himself on the sole chair the cabin boasted, he leaned forward, hands clasped between his knees.

"Yes, ma'am," he said. "This is rough on you. Now, I don't want to appear rude or cause you more trouble, but why have you come here tonight? If you want me to tell you what happened yesterday, you're barkin' up the wrong tree. I just got here a few hours ago myself."

"I know," she said. "That's why I've come to you. If you were one of Colin O'Doud's paid toadies, I wouldn't be here. But Benny swears you're not, and Mr. Ritter"—her husky voice broke. Osgood heard her swallow before she went on— "Mr. Ritter said your first official act as marshal went against the mayor's express instructions regarding the disposition of my son's body. I want to thank you for seeing him to Ritter's."

"You're welcome," he said somberly. "Didn't seem right to me." The woman was a mystery, he thought, as she reached behind the shawl with a sodden white hanky that stood out in sharp contrast against her black garb, and scrubbed at her face. She was as well spoken as any of the headmasters who, during his school days, had tried to pack learning into his head. They'd only been partially successful.

"It wasn't right," she said.

She had recovered from her tears, at least for the moment, and now he heard fierce anger behind her stoic façade. Was the anger Tompko had told him about on its way to the surface?

"Isaac was no thief, Mr. Osgood. They killed my son. Murdered him as surely as they murdered your predecessor. What's more, I think that since Isaac knew something about the killing, they took this route to make certain he wouldn't tell. More specifically, so he wouldn't tell you."

Startled, Osgood rose to his feet, the chair teetering at his heels. "Those are strong words, ma'am. Beside, it's been two months since Marshal Blodgett was killed. I've gotta say it's a bit unlikely trouble would rise to the top all of a sudden after this amount of time. Why now? Why would your boy wait so long to tell someone if he knew who killed the marshal?"

"Because he didn't know who to tell." She choked. "And because the girl who kept him here when Sean left is Colin O'Doud's daughter."

Black Crossing

Chapter 4

IN OSGOOD'S EXPERIENCE, there was no situation on earth more volatile than a pair of lovesick youngsters, especially if the girl's pappy didn't approve of the match. But would a father go as far as Mrs. Gilpatrick was insinuating? Was that what this was all about? Seemed a bit far-fetched. Besides, Mrs. Gilpatrick had made a definite charge regarding old Marshal Blodgett's murder.

Osgood could see she wasn't real pleased with him. Not after he'd told her he'd do what he could in finding Marshal Blodgett's killer, but that Isaac's case was more difficult.

"Tompko says a judge and jury tried and sentenced your son for timber jumping," he said. "They executed him. The case is closed. There's nothing I can do.

"And frankly, ma'am," he added, "without some kind of facts telling me otherwise, I don't have any reason to go poking into what's already done."

"What about justice?" the woman fired back. "Or doesn't that matter to you? Don't you care that a few people manufactured lies about a seventeen-year-old boy and then murdered him?"

He saw what Tompko had meant when he'd said Isaac's ma was going to be powerful mad. And she had the vocabulary to tie a simple man up in knots.

"Yes, Mrs. Gilpatrick, I care. Justice does matter to me." Osgood hoped he sounded soothing, even though in his opinion, her attack on him lacked a little in the justice department. "If someone can show me one shred of evidence the case was based on lies, I'll arrest the person responsible in the blink of an eye."

"What if the responsible person is the most important man in these parts?"

He took that for a challenge. "Doesn't matter if he's the president of the United States," he replied.

She was still as ice for a moment before she said, "All right, Mr. Osgood, you'll get your evidence. I'll show you the guilty party, then I'll hold you to that."

Osgood felt the pinpricks of her eyes from behind her shawl. Reaching behind herself, she opened the door a crack barely wide enough for a cat, slipped through and flitted away into the night, silent as smoke, all before he could get his mouth open.

"Wait," he said, a couple of seconds too late.

After she had gone, he tossed another chunk of tamarack into the stove, and rolled his two thin blankets out on the rope bedsprings. One blanket beneath, the other to cover him. He was apt to feel the cold tonight.

Some problems were best slept on, he thought. If he could sleep. As if he didn't already have enough to think about, Mrs. Gilpatrick had given him plenty more. What—or who—had she meant when she said, "You'll get your evidence?" He didn't like the sound of that. It struck him as chancy and dangerous. She'd best not mix in such things because she was apt to wind up getting hurt more than she already was.

Osgood blew out the lamp before he peeled down to his union suit and stretched out on the bed. He lay on his back, arms beneath his head, listening to rain drip through the hole in the low corner of the room.

Of course, the woman believed in her son's innocence. Who could blame her? It's what mothers did. And there was no denying the hurried way the boy's trial and execution had been carried out raised a whole lot of questions in his mind. Likewise, he downright hated that a young girl's name had been mentioned in connection with Isaac Gilpatrick. But neither of those things proved the kid innocent.

Complicated. The whole situation was rife with trouble. Osgood had the notion if he looked real close, he'd see a pit opening beneath his feet. Rolling onto his side so he faced the door, he did his best to force the sense of trouble out of his head.

"Think of the tall blonde," he muttered aloud. Magda Tompko had been a friendly face in a town that, on the whole, had received him coolly. He worked to recall what she looked like, what she'd said, and how she'd said it. Practiced small-talk, he knew that much. Friendly, like all good business people had to be. Tompko had said his ma was a widow woman. Now Osgood wondered if she was spoken for. He'd always been a sucker for big blondes.

But although he did his best to stir up interest in the fair, stately Magda, it was Isaac Gilpatrick's mother who filled his mind. Dark, slight, and mad as a wet hen. He wondered what she looked like beneath the coat and shawl she'd worn. He wouldn't even know her if—when—they met in daylight, which he had no doubt they would. One of these days.

"You'll get your evidence," she'd said.

***

IONE SLIPPED THROUGH the woods in back of the marshal's cabin to where she'd tethered her piebald cayuse. The path was slick with rain, and she fought to keep her feet in the wind and the dark. Once she fell to her knees, blinded by the storm and a tide of overwhelming anguish.

It was clear the marshal wasn't going to do anything about Isaac's murder. And regardless of O'Doud's kangaroo court, Isaac's hanging was murder in her mind, as surely as the bullet in Marshal Blodgett's back had been murder. The case was closed, Osgood had said. What would it take for him to investigate? Proof written down in O'Doud's handwriting? She wanted to howl at the injustice of it all.

A dripping tree branch slapped her face, the blow triggering memories of the night Isaac had been born. ti was on a night much like this one. She'd been alone, young and terrified, her husband gone on his regular Saturday night toot. The birthing was nearly a month early, and there'd been no one for miles around to call on for help. Sometimes she still recalled the pain. Pain. Had Isaac been that afraid? Had it hurt him that much? More?

She couldn't bear the thought of her child, the son borne of her body, suffering. Couldn't imagine a world without him in it.

A wild keening tore at her throat, losing itself in the sound of the storm.

"From what Tompko tells me," Marshal Osgood had said, "the work crew that convicted your son all had the same story. I reckon the jury couldn't do anything but bring in a guilty verdict. I'm sorry, ma'am. As sorry as I can be. It was one boy's word against four or five of Mr. O'Doud's men."

"They lied. They all lied for their boss."

Osgood had shaken his head, his hard-worn face doleful. "I wasn't there, Mrs. Gilpatrick. I have no way of knowing what went on."

Evidence. Ione had made her boast, and she intended to deliver upon it. And she knew just how she was going to proceed.

The rain increased as she reached her cayuse, the animal patiently standing with her rump turned to the storm. After untying the mare, she climbed into the wet saddle.

Tomorrow, after Isaac's funeral, she had a job to do. Then Marshal TJ Osgood would see. He'd have to see.

***

AFTER A MOSTLY RESTLESS NIGHT, Osgood overslept. His leg hurt more than at any time since the San Francisco doctor told him he might never walk without the limp. His head ached even worse than the leg, if such was possible. He needed to check the stove damper today, and the chimney, too, he reminded himself, blaming the headache on an unventilated cabin. As long as he was on the roof mending the leak, he might as well take care of all the maintenance problems. But first, there was the morning to get through.

He dug out a fresh shirt and shaved before escaping the oppressive atmosphere and heading over to the office.

A gusting breeze was blowing the clouds east into Montana. Clear air smelling of cedar and pine and the fern that grew on the forest floor helped clear his head. The marshal's office still held the wet dog odor, but Benny, in before him, had the door open airing the place out, with the fire started and coffee going.

"'Mornin', Marshal." Benny sounded a little more cheerful in the light of day.

"'Morning, Tompko. Cold today." Osgood shoved the dog away from where it sprawled half under the stove and filled last night's unwashed cup with coffee in which the grounds swirled. "I met your mother last night," he said.

"She said you came into the café." Benny's grin was sly. "Said you was a fine figure of a man."

Just in time, Osgood stopped himself from saying there wasn't anything wrong with Magda's figure either. His closely shaved cheeks warmed. That wasn't the kind of thing a man told a woman's son, even if it was true.

"I had a visitor at the cabin, too, after supper." He sat in the chair behind the desk, leaving the rocker, twin to the one in his cabin, beside the stove for Tompko. The straight chair was easier for him to rise from, considering his gimpy leg.

"A visitor? Who?" Tompko asked.

"Mrs. Gilpatrick."

Maybe Osgood put more inflection into that name than he meant, for Benny said, "Oh, yipes. How is she?"

"Let me put it this way. You were right. She's mad."

But Tompko hadn't quite meant "How is she," in that way, and Osgood knew it. Funny he hadn't put more thought into her feelings, and less into her stated search for justice. Still, he knew sorrow affected different folks in different ways. Mrs. Gilpatrick had given the impression she was more interested in vengeance than in inviting sympathy.

"Hope she's all right for the funeral this morning." Tompko's uneasiness on that score may have been because he didn't know if he was all right for the burying.

"She'll get through the funeral. It's the after part that'll be hard on her." Osgood's was the voice of experience talking.

Tompko had his eye on his boss's smooth chin, clean, starched shirt under his every day black coat, and the formal dark tie around his neck. "You going to Isaac's planting?"

"I'm going," Osgood said. "Might prove interesting to see who else goes—or who doesn't."

"Come to gloat, you mean." Tompko choked on a swallow of scalding coffee.

Osgood shrugged. "And I'm curious as to Mrs. Gilpatrick's state. I'm hoping she's calmed down some, by now. She was talking kind of wild last night."

"Calmed down? I wouldn't bank on it." His deputy didn't seem hopeful.

***

THE GRAVEYARD WAS a mile out of town, situated on the site of an old burn, in a meadow surrounded by leafless brush and a grove of cedar too small to be worth cutting. The cemetery already had a large population for such a new town, with plenty of cheap wooden crosses mixed with a few more permanent stone monuments. Logging, Osgood had heard, was a dangerous profession. Maybe more dangerous than being a lawman.

Ritter must have gotten up early for a six-by-three grave had already been opened, a bank of dirt piled at the edge. Together, the wind and sun had dried the topmost layer of soil. There'd been no attempt to pretty things up. It was a raw pit waiting to claim a body.

TJ Osgood and his deputy were the first to arrive, though not by much. A black horse pulled a plain buckboard into the meadow as they waited. Ritter was alone on the seat; a pine box rode in the wagon bed. Walking behind the conveyance was a slight, heavily veiled woman wearing a dark cloak, and behind her, Osgood recognized Magda Tompko's bright blonde hair beneath a subdued bonnet. A heavy-set older woman wearing a good black hat, and a tall, starvation-thin man added to the mourning party. That was all.

Not much of a send off, he thought. Was no one in Black Crossing even curious? Or was everyone afraid to show sympathy?

If so, who were they afraid of?

If he and Benny hadn't jumped to help unload the coffin, Osgood thought Ritter might simply have given it a shove off the end of the wagon, trusting the nailed down lid to hold the contents inside. As it was, the box wasn't all that heavy. Isaac Gilpatrick hadn't nearly the size on him his friend Benny had.

"Who's the skinny feller?" Osgood asked, as they lowered the coffin on straps into the hole.

"His name is Michaels." Benny grunted when they reached the bottom. "He's a lawyer, and also the closest thing to a preacher we got around here. Ma don't like him. I think he's on O'Doud's payroll."

After ten minutes, which the preacher spent moralizing on the wages of sin—heavy on Hades' everlasting fires—Osgood didn't like Michaels either. As for what Mrs. Gilpatrick thought, he could only guess, although, if the stiffening of her shoulders and the upward tilt of her chin was any indication, he had a good idea. She didn't say anything, but her shoulders shook. Ritter had soon had enough. He ahemmed out loud and picked up his shovel.

When finally the preacher stepped back, Isaac's mother moved forward. In a low, nearly inaudible voice, she began reciting the 23rd Psalm. About the time she came to the "still waters" part, Magda and the other woman joined in, adding a quantity of strength to the message. Benny recited, too, while Ritter's lips moved. The preacher was silent. He'd come to watch and to chastise, not bring comfort.

Mrs. Gilpatrick had a flower in her hand. Something red, vivid and living that she dropped onto the coffin as Ritter tossed in the first shovel of dirt. Magda put her arm around the woman's shoulders and spoke softly, and for a brief moment, Mrs. Gilpatrick sagged against the larger woman before her spine straightened again. Osgood kept thinking she'd throw back her veil now the funeral was over. That he'd get a look at her, but she didn't.

"You come eat breakfast," Magda said. "I bet you are hungry." She raised her sights to include her son, Osgood, and even the undertaker, Ritter in the invitation. She ignored the preacher and seemed to take the other woman for granted.

Mrs. Gilpatrick murmured something Osgood couldn't hear. Something Magda disagreed with, for she said, "You need to eat, yah, missus? Keep up your strength. To feel hunger iss not good for you."

"Thank you," the bereaved woman said softly, "but I must get home. I'm really not hungry, Mrs. Tompko. My thanks for coming today. I won't forget." Briskly, she swung around and walked away, the wind billowing her dark cloak out behind her.

"Rude woman," Michaels said. "Not even crying over the loss of her son. And no gratitude for charitable folks' helping hand at all."

Ritter paused long enough in tamping dirt on the grave to wipe a dribble of sweat from his forehead. "Don't reckon she has a whole lot to be grateful for."

"It'd be my guess she didn't like being told her boy was going to burn in hell," the other woman said. "I know I wouldn't. That was bad of you, Mr. Michaels. Real bad."

Benny whispered to Osgood that that the woman was Mrs. Tenney, Magda's business partner, and the café cook.

"I won't lie about what's so." Michaels sniffed. "She's got much to answer for herself, in loosing that evil young sinner onto the world."

"That isn't right," Magda said. "Besides, Isaac, he wass a good boy."

"He was a timber jumper." Michaels scowled at the women. "Mr. O'Doud's men said so, and the judge concurred."

Beside him, Osgood heard Benny beginning to breathe hard, a good indication the deputy was working up a head of steam. Best head him off.

"Come on, Tompko. We've got work to do at the office. Ladies." He tipped his hat to Magda and her friend, thinking he'd as soon be out of it, if the mood got too huffy. "I'll be in to eat later. Thanks for the invite."

"We'd better get back, too," Mrs. Tenney said, turning her back on Michaels. "Before old Shorty Krutzer fires my oven too hot to bake in, or eats up all my pancake batter."

***

IONE ESCAPED Benny Tompko's well-meaning mother, hoping the getaway didn't look like the flight it was. She appreciated both women's concern, really she did, but right now she was fighting to stay strong. Sympathy would only undermine her resolve. Breaking down in front of that ass of a preacher was a luxury she refused herself. He may have considered himself a man of God, but what she wanted was to tell him she'd see him in hell. Him and Colin O'Doud both. Odds were he reported directly to the mayor and she knew the mayor reported to the devil.

So she strode from Isaac's gravesite, head up and tough, when every atom of her being urged her to throw herself atop the coffin and grieve until she died, too.

Oh, Isaac, Isaac. How was she to bear this awful pain crushing her heart and assaulting her mind?

The only thing that kept her on her feet and moving was the oath she'd sworn on the red satin rose, so lovingly fashioned it looked real, she had let fall on top of Isaac's coffin.

I promise you, my son, I'll clear your name and see the guilty ones get their comeuppance. I promise you.

And she'd do it according to Marshal Osgood's specifications, too. Ironclad evidence of innocence, so there'd be no doubt in anyone's mind that her son had been a good, honest boy trying to do the right thing. Why hadn't someone protected him?

Why hadn't she protected him?

Ione Gilpatrick's vigorous stride carried her through the woods, oblivious to the bushes snatching at her cloak, or the small animals rushing from her path. Wind dried the tears on her cheeks. She had a destination in mind—a destination and a plan. She had an idea on how to go about finding Osgood's proof, but she'd best do it quickly, before she lost her nerve. Because to prove her son innocent, she had to prove another man guilty.

Hurrying now, she broke into a jog.

The cabin was only a mile or so from the graveyard, and after Isaac's funeral service, she reached it in less than twenty minutes. She paused there long enough to change out of her best silk skirt and heavy cloak. In their place, she donned a predominantly blue print dress, a white knit sweater, and a royal blue bonnet with a wide brim that shadowed her features.

If she were to be judged by her garb, she thought, looking in the mirror and pinching her cheeks to bring color to her pale cheeks, no one would take her for a grieving mother. These were the most brightly colored clothes she owned. Tears filled her eyes, but resolutely, she saddled her mare, blinked the tears away and set out again, this time riding the little piebald.

Instead of towards town, she pointed the mare due north, riding across country until she struck the road leading into the mining district. Isaac had showed her this shortcut only a few days ago, on their way home after he met her stage in Wallace.

"You better be able to find your way around," he'd told her. "To town and back, at least, for now. We'll need provisions before long, and you can meet folks then."

He had been a little embarrassed by the scarcity of supplies in the cabin, but she hadn't minded. It was a joy to see how her boy had grown. He'd become a man since the last time she'd seen him. And he had been just as glad to see her, a champion in his cause.

"I'm not at all sure I want to meet the 'folks' here about," she'd said, slicing a big potato into sizzling bacon fat and whipping up biscuits for their supper. "They haven't been exactly kind to you." That had been after she hired the lawyer to put down the false charge against him.

He had just smiled at her. "Everyone in Black Crossing isn't like that, Mother. Wait until you meet Benny and his people—and Selah."

Well, she met Benny, all right, and he truly was as fine a friend to her son as she could have wished. But on the afternoon Isaac led her through the same shortcut she was riding now, intent on introducing her to his Selah, the girl hadn't shown up at the meeting place. Ione and Isaac had waited an hour on a lonely side road. Isaac had been terribly disappointed, so much so he'd gone out again that night to see what had kept the girl. He had never made it home.

She shivered, the action on the reins causing the mare to break into a trot. Ione remembered how Isaac had smiled when he'd told her about meeting O'Doud's daughter on the sly.

"What are you doing to do if he finds out?" she'd asked, alarmed at the blithe way he believed he could outwit his enemy, as if it were all a game. Dangerous, she believed then, and how right she was.

Isaac had shrugged his unconcern. "He won't like it, I guess, but that isn't stopping me. And I can't let him or his men get away with killing Marshal Blodgett. You know that. Anyway, it won't matter what Mayor O'Doud likes as soon as the new marshal gets here. "

His recklessness had frightened her. She felt he put too much faith in a man he hadn't even met. "Have you thought about Selah's feelings if you succeed in putting her father in jail? She may not care for you anymore."

Not even that had dissuaded him in his quest to bring justice. "She'll stick by me," he had said, confidence in his young face. "Same as I'll stick by her."

The last time she had seen Isaac, she'd been standing on the cabin stoop, hugging the same sweater she wore now around her and watching as he saddled a sorrel gelding prior to riding out. He'd quit what he was doing and come over and hugged her. He'd smelled like a man, she recalled. No longer the boy he'd been when last they were together.

"I've got to do what's right, Mother," he'd said. "You taught me that a long time ago. Even if it isn't easy—or safe."

Well, it hadn't been easy—or safe.

Ione nearly missed the turn-off, even though she was watching for it. She sat still for a terrified moment, gathering all her courage before heeling the mare and riding up the long drive. The front door of the mansion—its formality incongruous in this setting—was open, but she ignored it and rode around to the back.

She'd be willing to bet servants in this house did not use the front door.

An old man came and took the piebald's reins.

"You the new housekeeper?" he asked.

Ione fingered the confirming note in her pocket. "Yes," she said.

***

OSGOOD WALKED AS RAPIDLY as his stove-up leg would let him, Tompko easily keeping pace at his side. He heard the females' voices twittering as Magda and the café cook followed them.

"Well, that was interesting," Osgood said.

"Interesting?"

"Yeah. She—Mrs. Gilpatrick—held her temper pretty well, considering. Don't know but had it been me, I'd've exploded in the preacher feller's face." Osgood bit back his smile. "Like the stout lady."

"That's Miz Tenney. She don't mince words none. She's a good-hearted woman, Marshal. She snuck Isaac and me cookies whenever she did the baking. Makes good gingersnaps."

Osgood was reminded of just how young his deputy was—and how young Isaac had been. Gingersnaps. Although on second thought, his deputy was probably better off eating spice cookies than downing red-eye at the Chain & Choker saloon, where, right this minute, he could see the bartender already unlocking the front door. The establishment opened for business early.

"Mrs. Gilpatrick..." Osgood hesitated. "That's a mouthful. I don't suppose you'd know her given name, Deputy?"

"Sure I do. It's Ione. Funny name, ain't it?"

"Ione." The name sounded downright musical to him. He grunted. "Well, it's one you don't hear too often."

Osgood sent the deputy on ahead to man the office, hardly expecting the duty to be onerous. In his experience, nothing much happened around little towns—even frontier towns—

except on Friday or Saturday nights. And, unless he'd lost count of days, today was Thursday.

As he'd promised himself yesterday, he went around to the stores where he bought a broom, lye soap, hammer and nails, and even begged a couple of rags from Mr. Bessinger at the general mercantile. Long as he was there, he also stocked up with a short list of groceries.

"Thought I might see you at the funeral this morning," he said, counting out change to pay his bill. "What with it being a local boy that died."

To which, the merchant replied, "I meant to come. Too busy." But his eyes avoided Osgood's as he spoke, and he barely prevented himself from looking over his shoulder, as though he was afraid he'd find the bogeyman there.

Same observation—same reply from the feller who sold him a dozen cedar shakes for patching the cabin roof. Dunfolk at the post office varied the response. He'd had a mail stage due, he said, but Osgood hadn't seen any such vehicle pass through town this morning.

He wondered if they'd all steered clear of the hanging as diligently as they had the burying. Somehow, he imagined not.

***

AN HOUR AND ONE smashed thumb later, Osgood was stubbornly hammering his newly purchased shingles onto his roof when he heard what sounded like a rifle shot. The report was louder and sharper than the crack of a pistol. Two more shots confirmed this impression. From his perch atop the cabin, he saw Deputy Tompko run out of the marshal's office and stand on the porch, looking first one way and then the other.

Knees creaking, Osgood stood tall, finding a better view.

He saw three men standing outside the Chain & Choker, two more outside the post office, one old wrangler with a pitchfork in his hands at the livery, and Magda Tompko at the café. All of them were gawking in the same direction—towards Bessinger's Mercantile.

Out of the corner of his eye, Osgood sighted a man on a horse walking straight down the middle of the street, his head moving right to left as though to see everything at once. He was packing a rifle across the front of his saddle. Two horses stood in front of the store, the reins being held by a stocky man dressed rough in cowboy duds.

"I'll be damned. A robbery." And here he was stuck up on a roof without his .44, or by preference, a rifle.

In his younger days, Osgood would simply have jumped to the ground. It wasn't more than ten…twelve feet, but with his leg only half-healed, he figured he'd wind up a cripple if he went with that stunt. He shimmied down the same tree he'd used to climb up and, hammer still in hand, dodged into the cabin to snatch up his pistol.

Seemed it took an awfully long time to him, but when he slipped in the back door of the office, Tompko was only just taking a rifle down from the wall and loading in cartridges.

"Marshal!" The deputy's voice squeaked, greeting his boss with relief. "Am I glad to see you. Couple of yahoos are robbing the store."

"I saw them. Two at the store," Osgood said. "Two for sure. There's a third." He discovered he still held the hammer, exclaimed in disgust, and thrust it into his waistband while he buckled on his gun belt.

"A third?" Tompko's face blanched, except for spots of red blooming on each cheek.

Fear? Excitement?

Osgood freed the pistol in its holster, and gestured his deputy nearer until they could both look out the door. "Feller riding down the road. Do you know him?" He was hoping, but Tompko shook his head.

"Watch him then." Osgood said. "He's another. Stay inside where you've got some cover. If they get past me and come this way, shoot at them from behind the door. But don't make a target of yourself."

"No, sir. Yes, sir. What're you going to do?"

Osgood grinned. "I'm going to stop them."

The man on the horse had his back turned for the moment, his attention taken up with watching the three citizens outside the saloon, whom he must have seen as the immediate threat. Fine and dandy, Osgood assured himself. Hope those old boys don't cut and run. He pounded across the street towards Bessinger's just in time to hear another shot.

The rider ignored the noise and didn't notice the marshal moving toward the store, but the horse holder couldn't help seeing Osgood rush toward him.

"Sam, law's comin'" he yelled. "Get out of there." He appeared of two minds on whether to mount up and ride, or to stay and fight it out.

By the time he made a decision, Osgood was on him. Without breaking stride, Osgood swept his weapon in an arc alongside the man's head. The would-be thief dropped like a rag thrown out of a second story window, collapsing in a heap with his revolver no more than half drawn from the holster. The horses, snorting and rearing, pulled the reins from the holder's nerveless fingers and ran off down the street.

Meanwhile, Sam, who must've had a clear view of the street from through the mercantile's open door, fired off a shot at Osgood. A bullet tugged at Osgood's shirt, a new hole the only casualty. The outlaw had rushed his shot and thrown his aim off. Before Sam could bring the pistol to bear a second time, Osgood skated into the store on his belly, sliding down the center aisle—which smelled pungently of pickles—like a train on tracks.

It was easy to see Sam hadn't expected that. He must've figured on holding the marshal at bay outside, where he and the rider could catch Osgood in a crossfire. Without letting him rethink this strategy, Osgood drew out the.44, and snapped off a shot. In return, the thief discharged a round over the marshal's head that came close enough to part his hair. Osgood's second bullet very neatly broke both Sam's wrist and his spirit.

The outlaw screamed, his pistol clattering to the floor.

"Mister," Osgood said over the noise, "you are under arrest." He was puffing around the words, what with running and then having the air knocked out of him in his grand entrance. He got to his feet at the same time the store window broke into about a million shards. The rider, he guessed, ducking. But, as the thought struck him that now he was the one in a trap, he heard the bellow of a second rifle.

Tompko, taking a hand in the fray and, as Osgood had instructed, firing, then darting behind the sturdy office door.

Osgood jerked the thief's good arm up behind his back and marched him over to stand beside the window, where he peered around the man's shoulder into the street. The rider was out there, racing his horse in front of the store and shooting through the broken window and in through the door.

Tompko held fire now, probably afraid of hitting one of the bystanders whose strong curiosity had kept them from seeking shelter inside a building.

Osgood put Sam between him and the street, Sam wailing that he was going to be killed. His protest landed on deaf ears. Lining the Smith & Wesson's sights up on the rider, Osgood called out, "Give it up, mister. I've got both your partners. Drop your weapon and we'll do this the easy way."

In answer, the rider snapped off another shot at Osgood.

"Ace!" Osgood's captive screeched as the bullet missed Osgood and blew the hat from his head.

Osgood twirled him around and shoved him farther inside the store for safekeeping. He fired a couple shots of his own, hoping to discourage the rider from lingering in the middle of town and shooting off his rifle in that careless fashion. Didn't look like anyone in Black Crossing had the sense to get out of the way.

Then, to Osgood's relief, the outlaw must have thought better of fighting it out, for he spurred his horse toward the woods, intent now on making good his escape.

But if he thought he could outrun a bullet, he misjudged the situation. He should've given up like Osgood told him. His horse was just building up speed when he rode past the marshal and right into the path of Tompko's next shot.

The outlaw threw up his arms and, knocked clean out of the saddle, plunged headfirst into the rutted, muddy street where he lay still.

Chapter 5

"WHAT'S THIS HAMMER doin' here? Looks like somebody dropped it on this feller's head." It was one of the sages from the saloon who asked the rhetorical question. Now the fracas was over, the elderly gentleman had ambled over for a closer look at the unconscious outlaw sprawled outside Bessinger's Mercantile.

Osgood bent and gathered up his dropped tool. "That's mine." He grinned, inviting the older man to share his wry mirth. "Thought it was my gun, until I discovered at the last minute it didn't have a trigger."

The sage guffawed. "Done a fair job just the same."

Sam stirred, moaning, as Osgood rolled him onto his back and retrieved the .45 the outlaw had been lying on. "You know him?" Osgood asked the sage.

"Never seen him before. Ugly galoot, ain't he?"

"I've seen prettier." Osgood handed the older man the confiscated pistol. "Here. Watch him for me. I'd best go help my deputy."

Tompko was leaning over the man he'd shot, and even from a distance, Osgood could see the boy's fair complexion going from white, to red, then back to white. When he turned green, Osgood figured he was going to puke.

"Huh!" His self-appointed helper took the pistol like he knew just what to do with it. "You sayin' you officially made that snot-nosed kid a deputy? Isn't he kind of young? Did a good job today, though, by cracky, for an office swamper."

What was the man talking about, had he deputized Tompko? Osgood froze, trying to hold his expression steady and keep his sparking anger from showing. Did that question mean what he thought it did?

"One of you men get the doctor—if Black Crossing has a doc," he told the other bystanders. "There's a couple of wounded men in the store, and I suppose somebody ought to take a look at this feller's noggin."

"Bessinger hurt? Who else?" the man he'd given the pistol asked.

"Bessinger's one of them. The outlaw, too."

There was a volunteer. "I'll get Doc Worthy. Hope he ain't drunk."

Osgood hardly listened to this spate of belated helpfulness as he walked toward Tompko. Deputy Benny Tompko, who was, as Osgood had expected, losing his breakfast.

The kid was shaking in his vomit-stained shoes when Osgood reached him. Too much to hope Benny had rethought the trick he'd pulled on Osgood, and that was unfortunate, seeing TJ felt a little proddy over the deception. But no, the trembling was more likely to be a reaction to his first time being under fire and at having to shoot back. In all honesty, Osgood felt the same thing, and he was no raw beginner.

"Tompko," he said, "you should've told me."

"Sir? Told you what?" Tompko gagged on another round of heaves, dry now.

"That you're a swamper, not a deputy."

"Oh," Tompko said. His eyes dropped. "That."

"Yes. That." Osgood knelt beside the outlaw, listening to hear if the man was breathing. He wasn't. No pulse either. Looking around, he saw they were drawing their own crowd of spectators towards them. They'd soon be surrounded. "So I'm hereby appointing you, officially, Deputy Marshal Benny Tompko of Black Crossing, and I'm making it retroactive to last night."

Tompko beamed, only to grow sober again when Osgood said, his harshness enough to quell the deputy's euphoria, "This subject isn't closed, Tompko. We're going to have a little talk."

"Yes, sir," Benny muttered, kicking dirt over the mess he'd made in the street.

Their talk was to end up somewhat delayed, what with Osgood summoning Ritter to take care of the dead outlaw, then supervising Doc Worthy while he tended the other two thieves.

Benny returned from helping Ritter cart the outlaw's body to the undertaker's shed just in time to lend Osgood a hand. Lugging the man Osgood had struck unconscious between them, they locked him and Sam in Black Crossing's single holding cell. Later, the outlaws could be transported over to Coeur d'Alene City with its bigger jail until they came to trial. Osgood hardly thought he'd be calling on the services of old Judge Pringle.

They threw a covering of mud over the dead man's blood, hiding the gore from every kid who came around looking for a thrill. The loose horses were rounded up and lodged at the livery.

Inside Bessinger's store, where he went to get a clearer picture of events leading up to the robbery, Osgood found the mister barking orders at his womenfolk. Mrs. Bessinger and her two daughters were hard at work cleaning spilled pickle brine from the floor, and picking shards of glass out of the shirts folded in the broken display window.

Osgood's next chore involved listening to Bessinger's account of the robbery. Turned out the storekeeper had only been winged a little, but it seemed the sight of his own blood had given him the shivers. He did plenty of yelling before his story got told.

"Wasn't long after you left, Marshal." Bessinger yelped as the doctor grasped his arm and swabbed the blood off with a cloth. "Man came into the store and ordered a slab of bacon and some coffee beans. Well, I went into the back room to cut the bacon, and when I brought it out, he had that new Winchester rifle I'd ordered for Hal Barton in his hands. He'd even poked around and found a box of shells and was standing there loading the rifle calm as potatoes.

"I says, 'What're you doing? Customers aren't allowed behind the counter. You get away from there and put that rifle down.' Well, sir, he just laughed." He broke off and squealed as the doctor poured some carbolic over his arm. "Ow, doc. Can't you take it easy? I've been shot."

"How did he come to shoot you?" Osgood asked.

"Well…" Bessinger's face twisted horribly as Doc Worthy wrapped a bandage around a shallow gash in his arm that had already quit bleeding. "Not so tight, doc. That hurts!"

From across the room, one of his daughters looked up from where she was scrubbing up spilled molasses and wrinkled her nose.

"Where was I?" Bessinger went on. "Oh, yeah. Well, he was standing there with the rifle acting like he was going to shoot up the stock. Smart alec young feller. I figured he was drunk. So I grabbed at the rifle, meaning to take it away from him, but lo and behold, if he didn't haul off and shoot me."

"I heard several shots," Osgood said.

"That was him." Bessinger's expression blackened. "After he winged me, he got a big kick out of shootin' everything in sight. For real, this time. The jar of molasses, that pottery pitcher and basin, the pickle barrel. I'll never be able to get the smell of vinegar out of these floorboards. So then, he cleaned all the money out of the till, and was just asking if I had any whiskey when you showed up, Marshal. Took you long enough, didn't it?"

Osgood didn't reply.

"Ow, doc," Bessinger said into the silence. "I'm a wounded man, not a side of beef!"

All in all, it wasn't long before the town was back to normal—or what Osgood figured was normal. Which was to say, quiet, the streets empty. Doctor Worthy explained this was due to most of the men being out in the woods. Things would change, he said, come Friday night, and stay that way until Sunday.

"You'll have no complaint about it being too quiet then." The doctor grinned. "And neither will I. Lumberjacks are prone to a powerful thirst. Then come the broken heads, the alcohol poisoning, the fights and stabbings. It ~~can~~ takes the rest of the week to catch up before the whole business starts all over again."

Noon had come and gone, with Osgood laboriously writing up the arrest and the death for his records, and to have on hand for whoever prosecuted the men. Marshaling, he concluded, was some different than reporting to his boss at the detective agency. He tossed the paperwork aside. "Time for a bite to eat," he told his fidgety deputy. "C'mon. My treat."

Benny perked up considerably at that, preening a bit when Osgood said, "You handled yourself well this morning, Deputy. Did real good. But you should've told me, instead of walking around wearing that badge and letting on like you had every right."

The deputy's pale skin washed a cherry red. His head hung. "Sorry, Mr. Osgood."

"What did you think? That I wouldn't find out?"

"No, sir." Benny swallowed. "I was going to tell you right off, but then…"

"You seemed to know your way around. What were you doing in the office, if you didn't have any business there?"

Stung, Benny looked Osgood in the eye. "I did have business there. Marshal Blodgett hired me months ago to sweep out the office, clean up after the prisoners and do chores. I just kept things up after he died is all. And I kept getting paid.

I even hauled a few of the drunks in off the street to sleep off their benders, just like Marshal Blodgett had me do. Nobody ever noticed the difference."

Osgood's lips twitched. His deputy evidently possessed a stiff backbone and a strong sense of duty. He couldn't help but be pleased. "Well, then, Deputy Tompko, go on with what you've been doing. Just keep me informed after this. Could've blown me over when that old duffer told me you weren't deputized. Can't say as I appreciated it."

"Yes, sir," said Benny. "No, sir."

Osgood shoved Badger away from Tompko's vomit-stained shoes and told the mutt, "Stay," in a stern voice. Wouldn't do Benny's reputation much good to have the stray sniffing after him.

Tompko walked down the street beside Osgood with his shoulders thrown back, chin lifted. Osgood was willing to wager the deputy was thinking he was a regular hero after the morning's events. And by gum, could be he had every right.

***

LATE AFTERNOON FOUND Osgood aboard a no-nonsense bay gelding he'd hired from the livery in town. He rode leisurely into the countryside, following Benny's simple directions to where he'd find Colin O'Doud's residence. The trail led him a half-mile east on the Wallace road, until he came to a path branching off toward a gap in the steadily rising mountains.

Osgood had left town early for his appointment, but he didn't head straight for O'Doud's place. Benny had drawn a map to where Marshal Blodgett had been shot last August, and told about how his body had been found hours later by a troop of soldiers from Fort Sherman out cutting wood.

Now, with Benny's map in hand, he followed the branch until he found the spot Benny had marked, a watering hole set in a small meadow a few yards off the road. Osgood whoaed his horse and dismounted, taking a game trail over to the spring. But although he poked around, there was nothing to be seen. A thick growth of brush had sprung up around some tree stumps. They were dropping their leaves, obscuring any evidence that might have been left from the murder two months ago.

He backtracked into the gathering dusk, glad he'd made an early start. He met no one, although in the distance, from over a ridge running roughly parallel to and southwest of the trail that Benny had marked as O'Doud land, he heard yelling and some sharp whistling. Loggers, he figured, directing the draft horses running the chokers in a skidding operation. Once, he was sure he heard a giant pine crash to earth.

O'Doud worked his crews hard, he thought. It was almost dark. Dangerous for a man to be swinging a double-bitted axe, felling trees at this hour. He felt hemmed in by timber tall enough to shade the sky. The wind sloughing through tree branches sang a sorrowful song.

In another mile, he found O'Doud's house at the end of a graded lane better kept than the streets in town. Lights were on in the two-story building, showing off a richly constructed edifice surrounded by dark woods. The house looked sadly out of place to Osgood, as though it should be bounded by others like it on a city street, with gas lamps and boardwalks out front, and maybe a rose garden at the side. O'Doud's place boasted no yard, no boardwalks, no paved pathways. Nothing but raw earth, slippery from yesterday's rain.

Osgood stepped from the saddle. Before he could tie the horse to the rail in front of the porch, an elderly man bustled around the side of the house and took the reins from his hand.

"Marshal Osgood," he said, rheumy eyes taking in the badge Osgood wore in prominent display on his coat lapel. "Mr. O'Doud is expecting you."

"I'm a little early, I reckon." Osgood took a gold watch from his vest pocket and opened the cover. "Fifteen minutes until six."

"Mr. O'Doud will want to have a drink with you before supper," the man said. "I'll take your horse out to the barn and water him."

Osgood nodded his thanks and mounted the steps onto the porch. In summer, he imagined, it would be fine out here with the drink the hostler had mentioned in hand. He'd make his coffee, and he'd sit in a rocking chair, surrounded by the cool of the woods and the scent of pine and cedar. But tonight it was only gloomy and cold. They could expect frost later on. Snow soon. He tapped the elaborate brass knocker.

At first, he thought the woman who opened the door must be O'Doud's daughter. The one Mrs. Gilpatrick had spoken of, and the one Benny had said his friend was crazy about. But a closer look showed this female wasn't a girl. She was small and as lithe as one, but as his eyes adjusted to the light behind her, he thought she must be at least thirty, maybe more. Pretty though. Was this Mrs. O'Doud?

"Ma'am," he said, snatching his battered gray Stetson from his head. "I'm Marshal TJ Osgood."

Her lips tightened. She drew breath as though she would speak, but then changed her mind. Opening the door wider, she made a gesture, ushering him inside. After they passed through the small foyer—Osgood leaving his hat on a mirrored walnut wood stand placed there—they entered a lamp-lit parlor. He saw she wore a plain black cotton dress, cheap and old-fashioned with a full skirt. She had a tiny white half-apron tied around her slender waist, an indication, if he could carry San Francisco manners to Idaho Territory, that she was a servant of some kind.

Maid or cook. Maybe the housekeeper.

Her hair, coiled in intricate braids around her head, was as dark as Osgood's own, before his became sprinkled with white. Her eyes were the stormy green of San Francisco Bay.

"This way," she whispered, as though reluctant to speak aloud in the hush of the big house. She led him down a paneled hall to a partially closed door and rapped on it. The door opened another inch, until Osgood could see Colin O'Doud seated behind a large desk with a map spread open in front of him.

At the slight sound of her tap, O'Doud looked up and saw Osgood. He laid a fat ledger book over the map and stood. "Come in," he said expansively. "Come in, Marshal Osgood. Sit down. Let me pour you a taste of fine Irish whiskey."

O'Doud seemed hardly to notice the woman, although in Osgood's eyes, she was deserving of a glance or two. "Bring a glass for the gentleman, please. Oh, and Mrs. Fane, set the table for four. I expect my daughter down to dinner tonight."

"Yes, sir." Mrs. Fane selected a pair of cut-glass tumblers from a fancy oak chest set at the end of the room and put one in front of Osgood. It was she who picked up the bottle and poured transparent amber whiskey into the glasses.

"Thank you," he said as she handed one to him.

She nodded, without once glancing at him, before leaving the room on silent feet.

O'Doud leaned back in his chair, his hands folded over his ample belly. It appeared to Osgood that the man had gained weight since he'd seen him in September, although he hadn't grown any more hair.

"How goes it so far, Mr. Osgood? I understand there was some trouble in town today." He sipped from his crystal glass.

"News travels fast." Osgood touched the tumbler of whiskey to his lips. It smelled smooth. Expensive. Delicious.

"I have people who keep their eyes on events in town for me. Generally, I know what's going on before the action has fully played out. "

"Is that right? Like hangings and such."

The words lay between them, cold as stones, and to Osgood's surprise, O'Doud merely shrugged.

"Like hangings and such," the mayor agreed.

"Then I expect you've heard my deputy and I stopped the trouble today before it got away from us."

"Deputy?" O'Doud settled in his chair and laughed shortly. "Benny Tompko? That's a joke, isn't it, Osgood? Tompko's still a youngster. What can he do?"

"I'd say plenty. He handled himself well today. I expect you've heard he's the one who killed the outlaw. Another burying the city'll have to pay for, but I reckon residents are glad it wasn't one of their own this time."

"Another?" O'Doud picked at Osgood's choice of words. He finished his whiskey and poured more, proffering the bottle.

Osgood shook his head. It would be best if he kept his wits about him, although the whiskey whispered a temptation. He raised the glass to his lips again, and licked away the single drop he allowed to spill from the container.

"Besides Isaac Gilpatrick," he explained.

"Why should the city pay for his burial, take money from the town coffers? That timber jumping young animal had relatives, or so I hear. Let them pay." O'Doud glowered at Osgood across the desk.

"Government always pays executions," Osgood said. "That's how it's done." There was no give in his statement.

O'Doud paused, his eyes narrowing, the lines beside his mouth deepening. His voice was chilly. "As you say, Marshal. I wouldn't want to argue over anything so insignificant. Yours is the voice of authority—in this case. Although, as mayor of Black Crossing, I've got to tell you I disapprove of the expense. And I don't appreciate having my orders countermanded."

Osgood raised the whiskey glass to his nose, inhaling the smoky aroma, saying nothing. He fancied he heard steel in O'Doud's words.

From somewhere in the house, a bell with a silvery chime pealed, calling the men to dinner. O'Doud led the way to a dining room furnished with ornate mahogany furniture and a table set for four, with bone china and sterling silver gleaming on a snowy linen cloth. It was the match of any similar room in San Francisco. A painting of a bird dog with a dead pheasant in its mouth hung over the sideboard. Blood dripped from the dog's mouth.

Funny anybody would paint a picture of such a hard-mouthed hunter, Osgood thought. Funnier still that someone else would put it in a place of honor.

O'Doud's foreman, Jensen, his hair slicked down tight against his head, a string tie around his neck was the fourth at table. He stood behind a chair, waiting for his boss. He and Osgood exchanged short nods.

There was a girl wearing a pink dress already seated at the table, her napkin open on her lap. As the men entered, her eyes flashed first towards him and then to O'Doud. He didn't figure it took a mastermind to know this was the big man's daughter, whom Isaac Gilpatrick had been sweet on. She was attractive, blonde, blue-eyed and vivacious, but he'd put money on her growing as stout as her father before long, especially if she bore a passel of children.

"I'm glad you took poor Isaac down," she told Osgood as soon as her father introduced them. "Even if Daddy didn't like it."

"Poor Isaac?" her father said. "You call that young scoundrel poor? He was on my property, Selah, stealing from me. I wanted him left on the gallows to serve as a warning to anyone else might be thinking of jumping my timber."

"Oh, Daddy, that's horrible." She flipped one graceful hand. "Anyway, you've got lots and lots of trees."

"Are you often bothered by illegal timber cutting, Mr. O'Doud?" Osgood asked.

"Not often. Word gets around I won't tolerate a man who steals from me. He tries, his reward will be death." O'Doud's voice was cold.

"Chancy taking the law into your own hands," Osgood said, mildly enough. "Are you sure Gilpatrick was guilty? He was young to hang, and most folks I've talked to say he was honest."

"He was caught on my property," O'Doud said. "My crew is hired to protect my timber. It's hardly my fault Gilpatrick was stupid, along with being young."

Osgood had a feeling the mayor wasn't talking about timber jumping. Or not entirely. And what about the smirk curving Jensen's thin lips?

"Isaac wasn't stupid, Daddy," Selah said, tears brimming in her eyes. "And he was honest." She turned to Osgood. "He was."

O'Doud tossed back the last of his drink. "Call Mrs. Fane," he told his daughter. "I want to eat my dinner in peace. I'm tired of arguing with you."

Selah, her mouth pouting, shook the silver bell sitting at her place. The resultant chime, same as the one that had called them together, summoned Mrs. Fane, who presently appeared bearing four bowls of soup on a tray. She served quietly, efficiently. Roast beef followed the soup, with O'Doud complaining the meat was too done, and the potato not done enough. Neither comment was true, and neither observation appeared to spoil his appetite.

"Pass the horseradish," he said, and Mrs. Fane hurried to obey.

Jensen never said a word, Osgood noticed, but shoveled food into his mouth as though stoking the furnace that kept his spare body chugging. It occurred to Osgood to wonder just what Jensen was foreman of. He didn't dress like a lumberjack, a miner, or a cowboy. What he looked like was a rich man's hired muscle, plain and simple. A bodyguard. One who wouldn't hesitate to draw his gun.

What, Osgood wondered, did O'Doud have to fear?

Selah ate steadily, until her full plate was scraped clean. She seemed unaware of Jensen's gaze locked on her every move—whenever he wasn't watching Osgood.

It was in the pause while Mrs. Fane cut a pie that ran with deep purple juice and portioned it out on plates, that O'Doud himself brought up the subject of Isaac Gilpatrick once more.

Osgood wasn't surprised. After Jensen's terse message last night, he'd thought there was more to this invitation than a simple social occasion.

"Jensen told me, Mr. Osgood, that you admitted Tompko had relayed my instructions regarding Gilpatrick. I find it interesting you chose to ignore them." O'Doud touched his lips with his napkin.

A nerve alongside Osgood's mouth jerked. "I uphold the laws of the land, Mr. O'Doud, and the rights of its citizens. My job is to preserve the peace and protect the folks who live in Black Crossing. Nothing more and nothing less. When I arrived yesterday, I found a situation that looked to step over the edge of justice. I corrected the situation. That's all."

O'Doud's face reddened. He started from his chair, changed his mind and sat again. Jensen had risen with him, his left hand going to his coat pocket, but O'Doud made a slight negative motion of his head. Jensen subsided, watching Osgood with the unblinking eyes of a predatory bird.

A buzzard, Osgood thought wryly. One who wore a gun at his boss's table.

Mrs. Fane poured coffee into his cup, the lip of the pot rattling slightly on the rim. Although she wasn't touching him, he had heard her indrawn breath and felt her body tense. A subtle indication he'd overstepped his bounds, perchance? He could have added that O'Doud's actions went beyond decency as well, but remembered in time that he was sitting at the man's dinner table and eating his food.

"Are you saying I was wrong with what I did?" O'Doud asked.

"Yes, sir. I reckon that's what I'm saying." He looked up at Mrs. Fane. "This is good berry pie, ma'am. Never had this kind before. What is it?"

"Huckleberry," she murmured.

"Well, that's plain enough." O'Doud's thin lips pinched a smile. "You should know the law better than I, I suppose. Seemed a good idea at the time. Discourage the rash of stealing we've had around here. I don't expect Gilpatrick was the only one out to steal his employer blind."

"I didn't know Isaac worked for you, Daddy," Selah said.

"Yes. For a while. I know he charmed you, Selah, but when I found him to be both a liar and a thief, I fired him. Believe me when I say we're better off without his kind in our fine town."

A glass slipped from Mrs. Fane's hand, shattering on the hardwood floor and making everyone start.

"Ione!" Selah exclaimed. "Now look what you've done."

"That was one of a set," O'Doud said coldly. "I shall take the cost of it out of your wages."

"Sorry." Mrs. Fane knelt, began collecting the shards. Her hands, Osgood saw, were shaking harder now.

"Putting a man's body on display smacks of vigilante justice." Osgood spoke to O'Doud, although his glance included Jensen. He calculated the note of disapproval in his words would draw attention away from the distraught housekeeper. "A dangerous thing to get started. Better to follow the letter of the law."

He watched as Mrs. Fane reached blindly for a jagged bit of glass. Blood started from a cut, although the woman seemed not to notice.

O'Doud shrugged. "Well, then, after this, I'll depend on to you to take care of such things."

"That's what I'm here for." But Osgood's response was absentminded. Selah had called the woman Ione. An unusual name. Too unusual to be a coincidence. That was Mrs. Gilpatrick's name. What was she doing here?

Chapter 6

OSGOOD TRIED not to let his expression change as realization of Mrs. Fane's identity sank in. The woman was stretching for a piece of glass near his boot. He toed it closer to himself.

"Let me help you with that," he said, reaching down.

She glanced at him, and only a sharply indrawn breath acknowledged his dawning recognition before she looked away. "I can get it. No trouble."

Yes. He knew her voice now. But what did she think to accomplish, here in the home of her enemy? Mrs. Fane. He supposed O'Doud had no inkling of who she was. Otherwise, the things he'd said about her son were too cruel to be borne.

Osgood itched to get out of this house, uncomfortable with the mayor's smug self-importance. He wanted Mrs. Gilpatrick out, too. It was a relief when O'Doud dismissed both the housekeeper and his protesting daughter, and broke out brandy and cigars. Jensen did the honors in passing the warmed liquor around. O'Doud cut the end from a cigar and lit it from the candle on the table in front of him. Soon, a gray haze fogged the chandelier overhead.

"What do you think of our little community so far, Mr. Osgood?" The mayor blew a wreath of smoke into the space between the men. Apparently, the brief spurt of animosity between them was to be overlooked, if not forgotten.

Osgood took one careful sip of his brandy, finding it smooth on his tongue. It was very good brandy. Too good.

He shrugged. "Most of these frontier towns are alike. A little wild, maybe. I've seen how hard it can rain, had a good meal at a decent café, and prevented a robbery. Oh, yes. And attended a funeral. The town, as a whole, seems fine."

O'Doud's eyes flickered at the mention of a funeral. "I hope it continues to appeal to you."

Jensen got up and refilled his boss's glass. Osgood put a hand over the top of his still full glass, and Jensen smirked. He hadn't, as far as Osgood remembered, spoken at all tonight, but his pale eyes watched everything.

"I'm riding a strange horse down a strange road in the dark. I'd hate to get lost," Osgood said genially. A puny excuse put beside such excellent brandy. He felt called on to expand it. "Best all around that I keep a clear head. I'll be starting an investigation into Marshal Blodgett's murder tomorrow."

O'Doud sipped his brandy. "Commendable of you, Osgood, I'm sure. But what do you expect to discover after so long a time?"

"There's always a motive behind murder, sir. Find the motive and you find the murderer." Things weren't quite as simple as he made them sound, but Osgood thought this was an approach that would spark a response from both men. He lifted himself from the comfort of the padded dining room chair. "And I'd better start back to town. Don't want to leave an inexperienced deputy alone for too long with those two desperadoes in the holding cell."

"Indeed," O'Doud said, his face calm. "Jensen…go ask Art to bring the marshal's horse around."

Five minutes later, the mayor accompanied him out the front door, where Osgood found the nearly invisible man-of-all-work had tied the livery pony to a porch railing. The gracious host bidding his guest farewell, he thought wryly. But he wouldn't call the goodbye friendly.

"A word of warning, Osgood," O'Doud said. "Make no mistake. Black Crossing is my town. I run it. You'll find, sir, that when I say how I want things to be, that's how they are. Don't ever go against my orders again."

Untying his horse, Osgood paused and met the mayor's eyes. "I always work within the order of the law, Mr. O'Doud. I don't know why you'd think any different." They were skidding around a situation that required plain truth.

"In San Francisco, when we spoke, you told me you ride for the brand." The mayor's lips thinned to a slash. "A cowboy terminology, I believe, that implies your loyalty belongs to the man who pays your wages. I'm that man, Osgood. My signature goes on your pay slip. That means you work for me. Remember that. In view of some of your personal problems, I'd think you'd be prepared to show a little gratitude to the man who hired you."

"Personal problems?" Osgood heard the strain in his voice.

"Your age." O'Doud paused. "Your love of liquor. I understand you once cost a man his life because of it, and lost a job yourself."

Osgood drew in a sharp breath. O'Doud had done his homework. Nevertheless, he dug in his heels, stubborn and not caring if it set well with the mayor. He saw now why the townsfolk had distrusted him. They must be used to O'Doud's high-handed ways.

"The chit that paid my way here says it came by way of the Black Crossing city council," he said. "That's the town, Mr. O'Doud. I work for the town."

"I own the town," O'Doud said again. "I own you."

Osgood gave a small shake of his head as he stepped aboard the horse. "Somewhere, Mr. O'Doud, you came up with the wrong idea. I'm not for sale."

He felt O'Doud's eyes boring holes in his back all the way down the drive, until the dark swallowed him. The livery horse, impatient to get back to the barn, walked fast, sometimes stumbling over the crushed rock that rolled beneath its hooves. Soon they reached the main road. He wished he'd had a chance to speak with Mrs. Gilpatrick. He would've asked her what in hell she thought she was doing, working for the man she swore had killed her son. It didn't make sense, unless she had revenge in mind. If that was her reason, he wanted to warn her off. Arresting a woman wasn't anything he ever looked forward to. Women were unpredictable.

Shivering in his thin coat—and reminding himself he needed one with a sheepskin lining if he was going to stay in this high mountain country, a supposition that was looking doubtful right now—Osgood chewed over some of the things the mayor had said. Anger grew inside him at the recollection, mitigated by a trace of satisfaction.

Some things were certain. Like O'Doud's dismay over Osgood not being the easy mark he'd believed. Or like Osgood's own resentment at O'Doud's knowledge that he had been known to like a drink of fine old brandy or smooth Kentucky whiskey just a little too much. O'Doud had apparently delved thoroughly into his past, yet hired him despite of it. Or maybe, he thought, because of it. Seemed a little strange to throw it in Osgood's face now.

The whiskey had betrayed him once. But only once. Booze had caused Pinkertons to dismiss him. One time he'd lowered his standards, and because of it, his partner had been killed.

Osgood kept his desire for drink in check—mostly. For years now, he'd succeeded, until he could sometimes forget the need had ever raged in him. Never again. He'd kept the vow he made all those years ago, but the brandy had been poison to his willpower tonight, pulling at him.

The evening was pitch dark, and although only about eight o'clock, it felt late to Osgood. He chuckled to himself. There was no denying he'd had a busy day. He smiled as he heard a coyote yelping off in the distance. Another answered from his side of the ridge, and for a few moments, there was such a cacophony of wailing a body might think all the demons had broken out of Hades. And then it broke off. Abruptly. Utter silence took over. Osgood reined the horse to a stop, though it tossed its head, wanting to go on.

"Whoa," he said, but soft and almost soundless. To his left, a bird shrieked. A fool hen, disturbed and roused from its nest. Blame coyotes on the hunt? Or something else?

After a bit, when nothing happened, he nudged the horse forward again. They picked up speed, but a sense of unease kept him away from the center of the road, riding instead on the verge where they blended with the trunks of trees. Every so often they came to a halt while Osgood listened. He had the uncomfortable feeling someone else was doing the same. Riding a way, stopping and listening, riding on. Mocking him.

How did the other rider manage to drift through the woods as quiet as smoke, ghosting along so only the wild animals were aware of his passing? The livery horse he was riding seemed loud, causing a scuffling sound every time it caught a toe on the tree roots rising invisibly above the soil line. Osgood reined the gelding in again, wary at the prospect of an ambush. One moment, he heard movement: a soft thud of hooves on the forest floor, a rustle of brush. And then nothing. The other man was copying everything he did, keeping track of his prey.

The gelding blew softly. Osgood jumped, startled at how the sounds, the dark, the feeling of threat made his blood run cold. He'd seen death already today. It was no stranger, brought home to lie at his door.

No use in turning back and seeking safe shelter from O'Doud. He felt certain of that much. Better to go on to town, he told himself, where there were lights and people. He clicked his tongue, signaling the horse forward.

The move saved his life. From close enough for him to see the muzzle flash, a shot slapped into the tree branch hanging a bare inch above his head. High, he thought automatically, tensing against the adjustment. The next one was closer as the shooter found the range. This one tore a chunk out of the gelding's mane. A third ripped through the skirt of Osgood's jacket.

The gelding lunged into motion as Osgood dug his heels into his horse's flanks. In the same instant, he drew the Remington Police revolver from his pocket. His backup gun, seeing he'd left his.44 Smith & Wesson in town as a courtesy to O'Doud and his daughter. A mistake, he saw now. The Remington was mostly noise at this distance.

There was a break in the trees. Osgood glimpsed the outline of a horse, a rider crouched on its back, racing parallel with him. He snapped off a shot, certain it did no good. The other man shot back, wide off the mark this time. Only luck would allow either man to hit the other, something their galloping horses and the night made unlikely.

More confidently, Osgood reined the gelding into the center of the road again. The footing was better here, and he was in less danger of being swept from the animal's back by
tree branches hanging low over the trail.

Osgood brought his pistol up, firing once, then again at the other man's horse running thirty feet away. Bring down the horse, and the fight was over. He had no hope of killing the animal, or for that matter, any desire to kill it, but the creature might lose its will to run.

He didn't hit the horse, but the man yelped and swore. All at once, Osgood's gelding was the only horse left in the race. He let him run for another minute before pulling him down to a jog, then a walk.

Fumbling in his pocket, he found a few loose cartridges and, hands steady, ejected the empties and fed the new into the Remington before stowing it under his coat again. The ambusher, whoever he might be, had been taught a lesson tonight. He had learned, contrary to what his eyes might have told him, that when TJ Osgood traveled, he was ready for trouble. Next time they tried to take him, they'd be more careful and better prepared. They'd be watching for his gun.

Osgood huddled into his coat, watching as clouds scudding across the night sky blocked his sight of the stars. Next time. What made him so certain there'd be a next time?

He shrugged, whispering an answer to himself. "Who knows?" But one thing was certain—he'd learned to trust his gut feelings a long time ago.

The lights of town had never seemed so welcoming as they did when Osgood came down out of the woods and rode onto Main Street. With a twinge of astonishment, he saw it must not have been as late as it felt because lamps still bloomed in nearly every window. Half obscured by curtains, a few heads were bent over a late meal at Magda's café. In Bessinger's Mercantile, it looked as though Mrs. Bessinger and her daughters were finally getting a handle on cleaning up the mess. He heard hammering out behind Ritter's undertaking shed, where the old man was readying the dead outlaw's coffin for burying tomorrow.

There was a light in the marshal's office, too, and after dropping off the gelding at the livery, Osgood made a beeline for it. He found Deputy Tompko there, drinking coffee and reading a tattered James Fenimore Cooper novel. Last of the Mohicans. Osgood was impressed.

Tompko looked up as the marshal entered, marking his place with a slip of paper. "Mr. Osgood. Glad you're back. How was your supper?"

"Uncomfortable...or were you talking about the food? That was fine." Osgood shoved Badger out of the way and stood warming his back at the stove. His cold, tense muscles began to unwind. "I can tell you that Mr. Jensen, for one, doesn't improve upon closer acquaintance. A cold fish if ever I saw one."

Benny grinned. "I could've told you about Jensen, if you'd asked." He pointed at Osgood's jacket. "What's that? I don't remember a hole being there this morning."

"Probably because it only got put there this evening. Somebody took a potshot at me on my way home. The coat was as close as he got." Thoughtfully, Osgood drove a forefinger through the neat, round perforation.

Benny whistled, which opened Badger's eyes and made his ears perk. "Looks to me like it came awful close, boss."

"Yeah. I kind of thought so myself."

"So, did you gun him down?"

"Not quite. Although it wasn't from want of trying."

Benny's expression urged further details.

"I may have done him a bit of damage," Osgood admitted. "Believe I winged him. I'll be making an uninvited visit out at the mayor's place again tomorrow. See what happens."

"You think it was O'Doud?" Benny sat straight up in his chair.

"No, no. Not O'Doud himself. Could've been Jensen." Osgood shook the coffee pot, found it empty, and resigned himself to going dry. He kept his own counsel regarding the argument with the mayor. "Jensen ate with us, but he disappeared before I left. He could've gotten ahead of me on the road, then cut off to the side before the ambush. 'Course, he might just have gone to bed, for all I know."

Benny's snort told what he thought about that.

Osgood grinned, but shook his head. "The shooter could've been most anyone. I didn't get any kind of look at him. Don't want to convict a feller without proof. Been too much of that around here already, if you ask me."

"There's an old logging road runs parallel to the main road to Wallace," Benny said, still stuck on Jensen. "It'd be easy for him to shoot from there. I'd better go out there with you tomorrow. You need somebody to watch your back."

Osgood yawned, fatigue and the dregs of battle excitement suddenly washing over him. "We'll see how it goes in the morning. One of us will have to be here to keep an eye on our prisoners. If we have any more owlhoots coming through like those we had today, we're going to need a bigger jail and another man to watch them."

"Got a telegram just after you left," Benny said. "From the county sheriff in Coeur d'Alene City. He said they'd send somebody up to get our prisoners. Said we did good work." His chest puffed out as he retrieved the note from a pile of paperwork on top of the desk and presented it to Osgood. "There was a reward out for Ace Donnelly. Turns out that's the one I shot."

"Well, now," said Osgood, barely glancing at the flimsy, "looks like you earned yourself a nice chunk of money, Tompko. But mostly, we just did our job. That's what we're paid for."

"Yes, sir," Benny said, his pride not deflated one whit by Osgood's prosaic tone.

The marshal checked the men in the jail cell for himself before heading over to his cabin. The man he'd winged during the robbery this morning was awake, his bandaged hand stuck outside the blanket. Probably throbbed like thunder, Osgood thought, not especially concerned for the man's discomfort. The feller he'd clubbed with the hammer slept, breathing loudly with a bugling sound. He hoped he hadn't permanently addled the man's brains. Better if he'd killed him.

"Take a gander at that man a couple of times during the night," he told Benny. "Yell for me if there's any trouble, and we'll call Doc Worthy. Otherwise, I'll be in early."

"Sure enough." Benny picked his book up again and found his place. "See you in the morning, Marshal."

***

OSGOOD ENTERED his unlocked cabin, appreciating the improved odor in a room that now smelled of lye soap and the outdoors. He'd had the place wide open for most of the day, letting the breeze blow through, while, at the same time, keeping the stove going. The result, as far as his nose was concerned, was almost livable. He didn't even feel the need to sneeze.

Leaving the door ajar, he struck a match and held it to the lamp's round Argand wick. Light flared, catching on Ione Gilpatrick's dark coat as she silently followed him in.

Or was that, he wondered, Ione Fane's coat?

Osgood straightened, shaking out the match. "Ma'am," he said. How had she gotten here so fast? He hadn't been expecting her at this time of night.

"I came to thank you, Marshal Osgood, for not giving me away tonight. I was afraid you were going to say something." As before, she remained just inside the door, away from the windows. "How did you guess it was me?"

"Stood to reason. I'd be surprised if there were two women named Ione in this town."

"Oh. So when Selah said, 'Ione,' the way she did, you knew?"

"Seemed likely. Come in, why don't you, and close the door. It's cold in here."

She didn't take him up on his invitation.

Without looking at her, he opened the front of the stove, shoved a couple pieces of dry wood onto the bed of embers and adjusted the damper. "This is a pretty good stove. It'll soon warm things up."

"But how did you know my name is Ione?" she persisted.

Osgood stirred, uncomfortable with the note of suspicion he heard in her voice. "I believe Benny may have mentioned it. Something wrong with that? What are you really doing here, Mrs. Gilpatrick? Or have you changed your name to Fane?"

"Fane was my maiden name."

He grunted. "You shouldn't have come. It's a long way from O'Doud's in the dark, just to say 'thanks.'"

"There's something else, too," she said. "I wanted to warn you."

"Warn me? About what?"

"Being ambushed. Although I guess you didn't need my warning tonight. I see you made it safely home."

A thought touched him. It could have been her shooting at him. He hadn't seen her when he left, but assumed she'd been in the kitchen cleaning up. If she'd rushed through her chores, she'd had as much time to get ahead of him on the road as Jensen had. The only question was why she would do such a thing. But then, why would Jensen? Of the two, Mrs. Gilpatrick had the stronger motive, if she was afraid Osgood would tell O'Doud that Isaac's mother was working in his house. Not that he intended doing any such thing.

His relief, when he realized it couldn't have been Ione doing the shooting, surprised him with its strength. Of course, it hadn't been her. He'd wounded the shooter, if only slightly. She didn't show any signs of being hurt.

"You shouldn't have come here, ma'am," he said again, "if you don't want to be seen." He stood in front of the stove, rubbing his hands together as the cast iron began to warm up. "Where'd you leave your horse?"

"I tied her to a tree, back in the woods a little way. No one will see her." Ione flipped down the shawl covering her head, allowing him clear view of her face. Her hair was coming undone from the coil at the nape of her neck. Dark circles were like bruises beneath her sad eyes, the lids swollen. She'd been crying again, on her way into town.

"I heard shooting on the trail," she said. "It was soon after you left O'Doud's place. Remembering what happened to Marshal Blodgett, I was afraid for you."

"Were you?"

"Yes. You shouldn't have said some of those things to O'Doud, you know. He doesn't like being disagreed with. Speaking out is what got both my son and Marshal Blodgett killed."

"Ma'am..." Osgood blew out a heavy breath. "Have you found any proof O'Doud is involved in Blodgett's murder?"

"Not yet," she said. "But I have Isaac's word it was O'Doud's men who killed the marshal. Why else would they do such a thing, except on his orders. And it was certainly his men who took Isaac and..." She couldn't finish the sentence.

"His men, ma'am. You said it yourself. Could be he had nothing to do with anything. Your son may have made enemies you know nothing about."

"Hah!" Her exclamation was tart. "If you believe that, you're of no use to me or this town. Another of O'Doud's henchmen, taking his orders and his pay."

Osgood's anger flared, until his good sense forced it down. He found himself making excuses for her. Of course she was upset. She'd buried her son today. Her pain justified her anger.

"It's possible you're right about him," he admitted. "But, ma'am, proof is required in a court of law. What you're telling me is hearsay."

"It's good enough for me. Just as it was good enough for the jury when they convicted my son." Ione's eyes burned into him, until abruptly, she sighed, shook her head and said, "For heaven's sake, quit calling me 'ma'am' in that smarmy kind of way. You already know my name is Ione. You might as well use it."

Osgood felt himself reddening, not quite knowing what to do with her invitation. "For one thing, ma'am, neither you nor Deputy Tompko have given a good reason why O'Doud—or his men—would want to kill Blodgett. For speaking out, you say. Speaking out about what?"

"Why, for the very thing he accused my son of," Ione said. Her words tumbled over each other in the effort to convince him. "Colin O'Doud was—is—stealing other people's timber. Isaac told me Marshal Blodgett had gotten a complaint the day he died. That he was going to investigate right after he got back from taking his prisoner to Wallace. Isaac, because he knows—knew—the country so well, was going to help him. That's why Isaac went there, to where the marshal was shot."

"O'Doud stealing timber?" Osgood couldn't keep the skepticism out of his voice. "Why would he do that? From what everyone tells me, he owns half the timber in this country as it is."

Her response was dry. "At least half. He wants the other half, too—and doesn't care how he gets it."

"Ma'am...Ione..."

He didn't get far. Her voice rose over his.

"You said you needed evidence...proof. All right. I'm going to prove it to you, Mr. Osgood. One way or another, I'm going to prove to you—to everyone—my son is innocent."

***

IONE'S SUREFOOTED CAYUSE picked its way along a trail lit only by starlight. The reins hung loose along its neck as Ione paid scant attention to where they were going. She relied on the mare to know the way home.

Home! How could it be a home without Isaac? Without a husband? Without anyone to care if she lived or died?

Of their own volition, her thoughts returned to Marshal Osgood and his thin, careworn face. The relief she'd felt when he kept her identity secret from O'Doud hadn't faded, even though anger crackled through her innards. Why was he being so stubborn? Why did he refuse to see? Stay out of it, like he said, and leave it to him?

She couldn't. She just couldn't.

And yet, in a perverse kind of way, she trusted him. Something within him drew her, like warmth from a fire. She hadn't felt this way about a man since Isaac's father—and maybe not then...she'd been so young. She wasn't sure she liked the feeling.

Isaac. Concentrate on Isaac.

Nothing else mattered, or so she assured herself.

Black Crossing

Chapter 7

"DAMN IT!" Osgood tossed his blankets over the rope bedsprings and surveyed the result. He'd meant to buy a mattress at Bessinger's store this morning, but the attempted robbery had driven it clean out of his mind. Now he was doomed to spend another uncomfortable night with a cold draft rising from the plank cabin floor onto his back.

I need a bearskin rug under the bed, that's what.

In truth, he was a little leery of shedding his shirt and britches before crawling between the two blankets, in case Ione Gilpatrick, for one reason or another, returned to plague him. She was getting real good at doing that—sneaking up on him when he wasn't looking. In fact, it was becoming something of a habit, considering she'd showed up here two nights running. One thing he could say about her, she was a pistol, bound and determined to do things her own way.

He banked the stove and, as a precaution, extinguished the light before skinning out of his trousers and climbing into bed. Old routine made him shove the pocket pistol beneath the rolled up coat he was using as a pillow, before he clamped his eyes shut. But, although tired after this long, eventful day, he couldn't sleep.

A funeral, an attempted robbery, a shooting—and another visit from Ione Gilpatrick. Thinking the day over, it was the woman who kept him awake.

Startled by the pop of an exploding pitch knot in the stove, Osgood blinked his eyes open, staring into the dark, where the only beacon was a slender edge of orange around the stove door.

He'd turned his back on Ione Gilpatrick for a brief moment, he recalled, and when he faced around again, she'd been gone. Faded into the night like a phantom, without him hearing a thing. She departed as easily as she arrived, which left him with a feeling of unfinished business.

If she'd given him the chance, he'd been going to tell her that, if what she suspected—if O'Doud had actually railroaded her son in order to cause his death—then she was playing a mighty dangerous game with her own life, walking into the lion's den. Trying to find proof, she claimed, but that was his job.

Problem was, where to start? Ione seemed to think he needed convincing that a rich man, a man with power like O'Doud, could be a shyster, but it wasn't true. He'd long since learned that the more some men had, the more they wanted. In his years as a Pinkerton, Osgood had discovered men who showed off the trappings of wealth were as likely to be dishonest as the factory worker or the cowpuncher next to him. As a lawman, he'd seen both kinds explode into sudden violence. Either way, Ione was better off staying out of it.

He would have to find her tomorrow and talk her into quitting, Osgood decided. If he could just get past her stubborn streak and her grief-driven anger.

***

DEPUTY TOMPKO WAS ASLEEP, his head pillowed on the desk, mouth agape, when Osgood opened the rear entrance to the marshal's office the next morning. It was early. The sun, not yet fully risen, barely touched the sky with color. Badger, desperate to get outside, heard the key in the lock and met him at the door, scooting out between his legs and nearly upending him in the rush.

"Place for a dog is outside at night," Osgood grumped as he shot the bolt behind him. "Can't keep watch sleeping in front of the fire." His ill-tempered words brought one of the prisoners to the barred hatch.

"Hey, Marshal, when's breakfast? Me 'n' Sam are hungry."

Osgood reckoned if the man he'd clubbed had recovered enough to complain of hunger, it was good news. Beating a man senseless wasn't something he enjoyed doing, even in the line of duty. It was only a little better than putting a bullet in him.

"I'll send the deputy for grub when he wakes up," he told the man brusquely. "Café isn't open yet. Don't seem to me you've done anything to work up much of an appetite."

The prisoner continued to whine as Osgood went about the business of replenishing the fire in the stove, and dipping water from a bucket into the coffee pot and setting it on the stove to heat. The marshal ignored the complaints. Meanwhile, Tompko slept on, the fragrance of coffee unable to reach him, until Osgood shook his shoulder.

Benny woke up slowly, like a child, rubbing his eyes and yawning. There was a red mark patterned in wood grain on his cheek where it had rested on the desk.

"'Mornin', Marshal," he said. His eyes bleary, he glanced out the window. "Something the matter? It ain't even daylight yet."

"I couldn't sleep," Osgood admitted. "We've got a few things to do today, Tompko. I figured we might as well get started."

Benny brightened at the thought of action. "What do you want me to do?" His face fell again when Osgood mentioned going over to the café and collecting the prisoners' breakfasts.

"Don't worry," Osgood said. "Your job doesn't end there. If you don't have a horse, I want you to rent one at the livery, and be ready to ride out with the deputies when they come to fetch our prisoners over to Coeur d'Alene City."

"Me? Well, sure, Mr. Osgood, if you say so. But I betcha those fellers can handle them two we got here. They ain't so much."

"Oh, I imagine the deputies can, all right. I doubt Sheriff Farnsworth hires on anybody incapable of doing the job. The prisoners aren't the reason I want you to ride along. I've got something else planned for you. Thing is, Tompko, it's a secret between you and me. Don't want you telling anyone—not even your mother."

"A secret?" Benny rose to the bait, neater than a cutthroat trout into the frying pan.

Osgood went over and shut the door separating the office from the prisoners before extracting a piece of paper from his pocket. He handed it to Benny. "Read this. It'll explain."

The document was a telegram he'd prepared. Benny read the blocky sentences once quickly, then again before looking up at Osgood. "So you did believe me. Me and Isaac's ma. I wasn't sure you did."

"I'm still not taking it as gospel," Osgood said. "But I was shot at by somebody last night, and I aim to find out who. An answer to this telegram should help give me a bit of O'Doud's background is all. If there's anything to find. When you get to Coeur d'Alene City, I want you to send this for me."

"From Coeur d'Alene City? But, Marshal, we have a telegraph office right here. It's right next to the stage depot."

"I know it." Osgood made no further explanation, although he watched as understanding gradually dawned in Benny's face.

"Oh," Benny said, "I see. You don't want anybody in Black Crossing to know. Well, there'll be something to find out, Mr. Osgood. Just you wait and see."

From the expression on Benny's face, Osgood could tell he was about bursting at the seams, holding back his, 'I told you so.'

Osgood ignored it. "I want you to stay in Coeur d'Alene City until you get an answer. Might be tomorrow, might be the day after, so be prepared to spend a night or two. The office will pay your expenses. I don't," he added, "want you riding home alone in the dark."

He sent Deputy Tompko off to find his breakfast then, and to break the news to his ma that he'd be gone for a day or two.

"Take your time," Osgood urged, figuring he could put up with the prisoners' yowling until his deputy fetched in their breakfasts from the café.

In the lag that followed, he took the time to write up an expense requisition for Tompko, ready to hand over to the city council as soon as he discovered who held the proper authority. In his experience, elected officials were fond of shunting such things aside. No novice to the whims of tight-fisted city fathers, he knew enough to have an answer ready in case one of the council members questioned expenses—and that included the cost of yet another publicly funded burial in the town cemetery. Mayor O'Doud wasn't the only one he had to please.

By the time he was through writing, with his figures done up in a sharp, tidy hand, and checked and rechecked, Tompko had returned with two steaming plates full of ham, eggs and fried spuds.

"Ma said to send you down to the café. She's saving some hotcake batter for you," he told Osgood.

Osgood grinned. "Bless her heart. I'm feeling a mite peckish, and that's no lie."

The prisoners were quiet, including the one with a cloth wrapped around his head, which made it easy to leave Benny in charge once more. Osgood's saliva watered at the thought of stoking up on Magda's good food. Hotcakes sounded just the thing, half a dozen of them smothered in butter and maple syrup. And a couple thick slices of that same ham the prisoners were eating.

Sunlight was filtering through the surrounding woods, promising a crisp fall day. The aspen leaves had turned gold almost overnight, Osgood noted, breathing in air laden with the scent of decaying leaves and burning wood. He headed towards the café, passing Bessinger's Mercantile, where the mister was already puttering around, setting out new kegs of pickles and crackers to replace those ruined in yesterday's holdup. Bessinger raised his hand briefly, acknowledging the marshal's presence.

He met Ritter, too, who was cutting through the alley between stores, headed for his undertaking shack. The old man unbent his stern demeanor far enough to cackle and remark, "Feel free to send another body or two my way, Marshal. Haven't been this busy since I left Eagle City. It's been a pleasure doing business with you."

Osgood just grunted.

The café tables were devoid of tablecloths this morning. The steamy room smelled of bacon and coffee, making Osgood realize he was ravenous. China thudded dully on the wooden surface as Magda placed Osgood's breakfast in front of him almost as soon as he sat down. She must've been waiting for him. Hot syrup steamed in the little jug she placed beside his plate. He slathered butter on pancakes and poured on the sweetening.

"Good," he said around a mouthful.

Her smile flashed. "Yah. Mrs. Tenney, she bakes goot griddle cakes."

"You ladies run a good business. Good as anything in San Francisco." That was laying it on some, Osgood admitted. Still, compared with like restaurants, it could hold its own most anywhere.

"That ain't what Mr. O'Doud says." Magda's smile grew wider. "He says this place ain't grand enough for him. He complains about the bad food, but he sure can eat." Her laughter trilled, making some of the diners look up in interest.

Osgood laughed with her. "For certain, he doesn't look like he's missed many meals. But don't let him fool you, ma'am. This might not be Delmonico's, but then, you wouldn't want it to be. You don't have any Rockefellers in Black Crossing."

"Magda," she said. "You don't call me ma'am."

"Magda."

He could tell she'd never heard of Delmonico's. Or Rockefeller either. Mention those names to Ione Gilpatrick, though, and he bet she'd know who he was talking about. Ione was out of place in Black Crossing, like a cactus stuck in amongst all these pine trees. Just about as prickly, too. It was Magda who belonged here. As she moved to refill another customer's coffee cup, he heard her speaking to the man, a lumberjack, or so he assumed from the man's attire. Hard to miss the calked boots. Magda addressed him in a language other than English. Finnish? he wondered, taken by the lilting cadences. Definitely Scandinavian.

***

HIGH NOON HAD COME and gone before the deputies out of Coeur d'Alene City departed Black Crossing with the prisoners. Benny, mounted on the same rented horse Osgood had used the previous night, rode shotgun behind them, appearing about as officious as any experienced bureaucrat.

Osgood grinned as Benny saluted him with a cocky farewell gesture full of hidden

meaning. The deputy's wide face was flushed with excitement—or maybe it was embarrassment, seeing his ma came out of the café to shout last-minute advice as she watched him leave.

The marshal's grin quickly faded as he discovered Magda was not alone in observing the little cavalcade. Standing beneath the overhang at the telegraph office, Colin O'Doud made his own observations. O'Doud was alone. Jensen, his foreman, was conspicuous by his absence.

The brief excitement over, the town soon fell quiet. Osgood, killing time until he deemed the signs propitious in following O'Doud as the mayor rode home, dropped in at Bessinger's and ordered himself a cheap mattress and a feather pillow to be delivered to the cabin.

"The mayor was in a bit ago," Bessinger said, laboring over writing up the receipt for Osgood's purchases. "Me and Dunfolk and Harvey Leonard from the livery—we're council members—met with him. Got him to sign off on paying Ritter for those funerals. By golly, I'd never've thought you'd pull that off, Osgood. Black Crossing is footing the bill for the Gilpatrick doings."

"It's only right," Osgood said. "I reckon Mr. O'Doud saw that."

Bessinger shook his head. "He agreed to pay Tompko deputy wages, too, instead of swamper pay. Guess he figured he had to after the kid saved my bacon yesterday. Well, between you and Tompko both. But O'Doud is a thinker, and that's no lie. The outlaw Tompko killed was riding a pretty fair horse, so the town confiscated it. Gonna sell it, and pay for Ace Donnelly's burial out of the proceeds."

"Smart," Osgood said. To give the man his due, O'Doud had some decent ideas when it came to running the town.

Osgood had seen the aforementioned horse corralled over at the livery. It was a good one, which set wheels turning in his own mind. Consequently, his next stop was the livery. With Harvey Leonard, the proprietor, beside him, he set his sore leg on the bottom rail of the pole corral fence where the outlaw's horse was confined, and studied the animal. It was a gelding, plain chocolate brown in color, rangy, with good-sized feet suitable for covering a lot of rough ground. It snorted when it saw Osgood, but didn't shy away from his hand.

"How much?" Osgood asked.

Harvey Leonard rolled the sprig of dried grass he was chewing from one side of his mouth to the other. "I can let him go for forty-five dollars."

Osgood gave the hostler a bug-eyed stare. It was better than half of his first month's salary. "I guess you can!"

Leonard shrugged. "Gotta cover the expenses of plantin' that outlaw. And then, I'm entitled to a little somethin', ain't I?"

"Depends on what you think of as little. Seems to me our view might differ a hair." The gelding impressed Osgood, though, with his kind eye and fine, smooth action as he trotted around the corral. The lawman made as if he'd lost interest and moved toward a hammer-headed roan standing hipshot off by himself.

"Tell you what," Leonard said, interrupting the motion. "You try the gelding out. Take him for a ride and see if you like him. If you do, pay me the forty-five dollars and I'll throw in the saddle and bridle. That's fair. Don't leave me much, but shoot, I ain't had the keep of him for long."

Osgood turned back and considered the animal again. He made a show of thinking the offer over. "All right," he said, drawling his response out slow. He made it sound like Leonard had forced him into it. "I'll give him a try. But I'm not promising anything. I've got other business, but if you'll rig him out, I'll be back in about an hour."

Worst thing a feller could do when horse trading was to appear too eager.

"I'll have him saddled," Leonard promised.

Osgood hid his grin on the way back to the office. Once there, he propped his feet on the desk and napped for the hour. In truth, he didn't have a thing to do, except let O'Doud get a head start. Oh, yeah. And make certain Badger wasn't locked up inside the jail.

***

MID-AFTERNOON FOUND Osgood stopped in the road, in the exact spot where he'd been fired on, last night. He was sure of the location because he remembered the low-hanging branch that had nearly swept him from his horse in the first startled moment. Daylight didn't improve the area much. It was still dark beneath the trees. Dark, cold, and dank. And silent. Osgood had a twitch between his shoulder blades, like a horse shaking flies from its hide.

Tompko had told him there was a logging road running parallel to the main road, and he'd seen the tracery of it for himself on the county map pinned to the wall inside the mercantile. He urged the gelding through trees and brush until he found the trail for himself. Tompko had said no one used this route anymore, but there were fresh tracks here. One set since the rain, stamped clearly into the clay, all jumbled up where the bushwhacker had waited. There was an empty Bull Durham sack, too. There'd been a tag hanging out of Jensen's shirt pocket last night, he recalled. But then, it was the tobacco of half the men in the country who smoked favored, including himself on occasion. This one could've belonged to anybody.

The gleam of a shell casing caught Osgood's eye. Stepping from the saddle, he bent down and picked it up, finding it to be a .44/40. A good many of the men around this neck of the woods probably owned the same caliber rifle. There might be lots of spent shells scattered around where men had been hunting. But they weren't the ones kicked out where the first shot aimed at him had come from. And the brass on the one in his hand was bright and new.

That's all the shell told him, though. He wasn't much smarter now than when he'd started. He walked on, leading the horse, his eyes intent on the ground. What was he looking for anyway, he asked himself? A placard that said, "Jensen was here" would help. Or maybe just sign with enough individuality he could pinpoint one specific person.

Aware of the shadows already closing in, he knew the afternoon was running out. Soon, it would be too dark to see.

The sighing between the treetops created a living sound through the timber. Chipmunks scampered back and forth across the trail. Birds called and squawked. Once, down at the bend in the road, a whitetail—a big, six-point buck—dashed into plain sight, swerved abruptly, then disappeared into the woods. Small animals, as at a signal, fell silent.

Osgood's senses stretched, going into high gear. He heard the muffled thud of a horse's hooves on the forest floor. Reaching for his gun, he took out the.44 and cocked it.

The hoofbeats came nearer, just around the bend where the deer had fled. He rested the pistol barrel on his forearm, certain he wouldn't be taken by surprise this time.

But he was mistaken. The rider did surprise him.

Chapter 8

"WHAT ARE YOU DOING HERE?" Relief roughened Osgood's voice as he asked the question. As though frozen, his finger still curled stiffly around the.44's trigger. He'd come within a hair of snapping off a shot.

Ione Gilpatrick continued on, riding toward him until their horses were only a few feet apart. She leaned back on the reins, eyed the pistol pointed in the vicinity of her heart, and arched her brows. "You can put the gun away, Marshal Osgood. I'm no threat to you."

Osgood breathed in deeply through his nose, and let down the hammer. "That is a matter of opinion, ma'am," he said. "You didn't answer my question."

"Have you forgotten, Marshal? I work for Colin O'Doud. I'm on my way there now."

The pistol hovered a few seconds more before he slid it into the holster. This is what he'd wanted to discuss with her, only he hadn't thought the meeting would take place here in the woods.

"This job of yours is something we're going to talk about, Mrs. Fane," he said. "I believe it's time you quit."

Her chin came up. "That's where you and I differ. Last night, you told me you require proof of O'Doud's complicity in Isaac's murder. So, Marshal, if that's what it takes, I'll quit when I've found your proof. Not before."

A muscle in Osgood's jaw clenched. "Are you saying it's my fault, what you're doing?"

She remained silent, her sea-dark eyes meeting his.

Yes, he answered his own question. That's what she was saying. Just not out loud. She must still question if he was O'Doud's man, in which case, she was a brave woman to have faced his drawn gun and said what she did. Brave—or foolish.

"You don't know there's anything to find," he said, trying to instill a modicum of reason into her head. "What would there be? Do you expect to unearth documents with a confession written on them? Unlikely."

"I don't know what I expect. Something. Isaac told me what he saw when Sheriff Blodgett was murdered." She edged her cayuse, a long-eared, jug-headed runt not much bigger than a child's pony, closer to where he stood. With him standing on the ground, she wasn't much higher than he. "Somewhere there must be proof. Tell me what you need and I'll look for it."

"Has it occurred to you there might just have been bad blood between a man who didn't want to lose his daughter, and the lad who's was wooing her?"

"Are you insinuating Isaac said what he did because he was irked with O'Doud?" There was outrage in Ione's voice. "That's ridiculous. And my son is dead. Rather a drastic reaction, don't you think?" She choked on a suppressed sob—or her anger.

Well, yes, Osgood conceded. Put that way.

"What if your suspicion of this man is correct?" He heard the antagonism in his tone, part of it aimed at himself as he realized he, too, believed O'Doud as guilty as Ione said he was, even without proof. "Do you realize the danger you're putting yourself in? I can't protect you if I can't see you, ma'am. And if neither Sheriff Blodgett nor your son could help themselves, what makes you think you can?"

Her words were quiet. "It doesn't matter about me. I don't care. Isaac was all I had in this world, Mr. Osgood. My only child. Do you have any idea how a mother feels when her child dies? Can you imagine how it feels to know he was murdered? I don't have words enough to tell you."

He knew how it felt to lose a partner. Or a parent, or a brother. That was bad enough.

"No, ma'am," he said, in unwilling consideration. "I don't suppose I do know how you feel. But I care about you. You matter to me."

As though she hadn't heard him, Ione struggled to explain. "It was Isaac and me together against the world, after my husband died. He left us nothing except debts. A wild Irishman, tried and true, drunk every Saturday night and good for nothing on Sunday. When he was gone, it was iffy sometimes, just putting food on the table. Then I got the job teaching at a girl's school in Denver. I had to live in, and my employers wouldn't allow Isaac to stay with me."

Osgood stepped closer to Ione, reached up, and lifted her from the sidesaddle. She was light, just a little bit of a woman. She had a faraway look on her face, as though she wasn't aware of dismounting, of standing with his hands on her arms. He found himself reluctant to release her for fear she'd collapse.

"But Isaac's Uncle Sean had been pestering for the care of the boy," she went on. "I've never known why, except maybe to make me more miserable. And so, against my better judgment, I let my son go. To this. To his death. While I paid off his father's debts." There was a wealth of bitterness in those last few words. And rage. He heard it, tightly banked.

"Ma'am...Ione..." Osgood couldn't imagine feeling any more helpless. "It wasn't your fault."

A tracery of tears spilled down her cheek. "No. And yes. But after Isaac, it's me who pays. And pays and pays."

If Osgood could have put a color to her words, the color would have been white. White—or maybe transparent. Leached of everything except pain. He found himself patting her on the back, until she stiffened and pulled away from his clumsy attempt at sympathy.

"Colin O'Doud is not going to get away with it," she said, squaring her shoulders. "Whatever else, he's not going to kill my son and walk away free."

"No, he's not," Osgood agreed, "if he did what you think he did. But proving, or disproving, his innocence is my job, not yours. That's why I'm here, and that's why you're leaving. You're going home, right now."

He didn't know where she lived, he realized. Benny's directions had pointed toward a cabin a mile or so out of town. A place secluded enough no one had ever visited her that he'd heard of, aside from Benny Tompko, who had gone there with Isaac. And when she'd come to the funeral, she'd been bundled up so no one even knew what she looked like.

"Home." She snorted. "I most certainly am not. It's not that I don't trust you to do the best you can, Mr. Osgood, but I've established an excuse to be on O'Doud's premises. I'm one of the hired help. There's no reason to suspect me of anything. You, on the other hand, have already been shot at. Show up anywhere around his place, and the next time might be fatal. Just like it was for Sheriff Blodgett."

"I'm hard to kill."

Her skin, stretched tautly over high cheekbones, paled. "Those were my son's exact words, the last time we spoke."

"Nevertheless, I can't let you—"

"You can't stop me. What are you going to do? Tell him who I am? Put me in jail?" She sounded scornful, disbelieving.

"I might jail you," he said grimly. "Protective custody, they call it."

She studied him, as though wishful of arguing more, but she already had him over a barrel, and that was the truth.

The ghost of an unexpected smile tilted one side of her mouth. "No, you won't. You said I could trust you. You said you cared what happened to me. O'Doud would find some way to get rid of me, too, if you told him who I am, and you know it. So I'll carry on, Marshal, just as I intended to do all along. I will do this, however. If I find out anything, I'll report directly to you."

Stubborn woman! Exasperated, Osgood whipped off his hat and beat it against his thigh, then jammed it on his head again. "Is that supposed to ease my mind? Well, it doesn't."

"I'm sorry."

She wasn't sorry at all, and he knew it. As she was well aware. Almost as though she was retreating, she climbed back onto her horse.

"Your name," she said, out of the blue as she watched his face. "What is it? TJ must stand for something."

He wondered who had told her his name. He never had. "Just letters of the alphabet, ma'am. They don't mean anything."

"You called me Ione a moment ago. If I'm going to call you TJ, I guess you'd better drop the ma'am thing permanently."

She was a trial, for certain. Tricky and slippery, and could tie him in knots, old as he was—as old as she was—without half trying. Enough so that he forgot to voice another protest as he watched her pony's narrow hindquarters shuffle off down the road. The horse, he noted automatically, was knock-kneed.

Osgood found three more .44/40 cartridge casings, the brass bright amidst the dark soil and dropped pine needles of the trail. The casings were spaced appropriate to where he recalled he'd been when the bushwhacker shot at him. The shells had obviously been fired since the rain. When he picked up the last one, he also found a few drops of dried blood nearby. He had hit the shooter, as he'd thought, just not hard enough to bring him down. Startled him enough Osgood had had a chance to get away. A piece of luck.

A thought struck him. At least he could ask Ione, next time they met, if Jensen was sporting any kind of wound. And maybe what, if anything, Selah O'Doud had to say about her father's business. The girl had seemed almost confrontational last night. The question would give him an excuse to go looking for Mrs. Gilpatrick, and another chance to talk her into leaving here. Leave not only O'Doud's employ, but also the whole of Idaho Territory.

Well, he could try anyway. But remembering the bleak look in her eyes, he didn't know how successful he'd be.

He'd like to send her down to San Francisco—except O'Doud had ties there. That was where he'd gone when it came time to hire a new peacekeeper for Black Crossing. Better yet, for Ione, might be Sacramento. Osgood had a little house there, inherited from his mother. He hadn't been around in a number of years to inspect its condition, but he knew the place was habitable.

Yes. He'd put her on the train and send her to Sacramento. Make her go.

The abandoned logging road was a dead end. Osgood followed Ione at a distance, watching, when they got to O'Doud's place, until he saw the old man come from the barn, take her horse, and lead it away. Ione, entering through the back door, went into the house and shut it behind her without a backward glance.

Osgood saw nothing to alarm him. No bands of rough-looking characters standing by with axes or chains. No gunmen with low-slung holsters. Only a quiet country house, out of the ordinary only in its size and style. If there was anything here to prove O'Doud a killer, it wasn't sitting out in the open.

***

IONE WAS HANDING her mount off to O'Doud's wrangler when the question of why Marshal Osgood—TJ—had been lurking on the trail out back of the mayor's place occurred to her.

He was doing more of his evidence gathering, she supposed. Trying, at least. Much good it would do him if he didn't live long enough to put what he learned to use. He'd had his gun drawn, though, when she appeared and, from his grim expression, been ready to use it. Far from being an easy target, it appeared he was on the lookout to prevent a bullet in the back like Marshal Blodgett had gotten. Apparently, her warning had struck home.

But he was being discreet and taking her safety into account, as well. Bless him for that. It was enough to make her shake with relief.

Slipping through the open back door of the O'Doud mansion, she took off her sweater and donned a fresh white apron before beginning her work. No guests were expected for the evening meal, unless plans had changed since last night, but she'd already discovered both the mayor and his daughter were fussy, although hearty eaters.

She'd bake a custard pie she decided, and went outside to fetch eggs and milk from the springhouse. When she returned, hands full, Jensen was sitting at the kitchen table, a cup of coffee in front of him, obviously waiting for her. Her insides clenched.

"Mrs. Fane…"

He was dry-washing his hands, then stretching out his fingers and shaking them in a motion she concluded was meant to keep them supple. And quick, she supposed. Important for a gunfighter. Dangerous for his opponent.

"Mr. Jensen," she replied. Holding herself steady took effort.

"I seen you come in on the trail through the woods."

"Yes. It's the shortest route from my house," she said, then wished the words back in her mouth. No use giving him a clue where she lived—the same as where Isaac had lived.

Ignoring him, she sat her burden on the work table, found an earthenware bowl and began cracking eggs into it. He observed her busyness like a high-flying hawk watches his prey on the ground, ready to strike as soon as it showed signs of escaping. His regard was unnerving.

"That can be a dangerous trail at night," he persisted. "Reckon I should see you home tonight. Make sure you get there all right." He never blinked.

"It's not far once I reach the road." She avoided his gaze. "I'm used to doing for myself." She was trembling as she fished a chunk of shell out of the bowl before beating the eggs with a wire whip. A pinch of salt went into the pale gold froth, a little white sugar flavored with a vanilla bean, some rich whole milk. A skiff of nutmeg.

"How far—exactly? Think I might come visiting some evening, Mrs. Fane. You'd be glad of that, wouldn't you?"

"I prefer my own company." Her reply would have driven most men away. Not him. He merely flapped his hands again and stared unnervingly at her.

Ione left the custard and fled into the pantry where she took her time collecting flour and lard for pie crust. If she ignored him, maybe he'd go away.

But he didn't. When she returned to the worktable with her supplies, he was there, leaning against the door jamb, watching her with a knowing grin twisting his thin lips. He knew she was afraid of him and reveled in it, she thought, hating him.

"Get out of my kitchen, Mr. Jensen," she said. "I'm busy." The frost in her voice would have frozen tree sap, but it had no discernable effect on Jensen. "I can't work with you in my way. Mr. O'Doud is going to want his dinner on the table on time, and this pie for dessert."

He stalked her like a wildcat stalks a rabbit, until he was close enough to lay an arm across her stiff shoulders.

"Do I bother you, Mrs. Fane?"

A quiver shook her body, answer enough if he had wit to sense it. Revulsion. A longing for Marshal Osgood to come riding to her rescue surprised her with its intensity.

His thin lips snarled upward. "You tremble, Mrs. Fane. Is that because you want me to visit, I wonder? Or because you don't?" His voice dropped. "Are you afraid of me?"

Ione's tongue was curled in the roof of her mouth. She didn't answer, didn't look up from the pie crust she kept working and working, until it was sure to be tough as shoe leather.

"What are you afraid of?" he asked.

Ione had never in her life been so glad to see a person as she was to see Selah waltz through the kitchen door carrying a frilly petticoat over one arm and a sewing basket over the other.

"Mrs. Fane, could you mend this for me before tonight?" she asked, her sharp eyes taking in the tableau of her housekeeper standing frozen with the foreman breathing in her ear.

Ione jerked away. Jensen's arm fell to his side. "Of course," she said, maybe a little too heartily. "I'll be glad to."

Selah pursed her mouth. "My father was looking for you earlier," she told Jensen. "Something about a message he wants carried out to the logging camp. He left a note in his office for you."

Languidly, Jensen straightened. "Sure thing, Miss Selah." But he didn't leave right away. Before she could look away, he caught Ione's eye. "Watch for me," he said. "I'll be coming for you one of these days."

Only then did he slouch off. Was she mistaken, Ione wondered, or was he favoring his right leg the slightest bit?

Selah gave Ione an odd look, but all she said was, "Just put the petticoat in my room when you're done, Ione."

***

OSGOOD DELAYED HIS ARRIVAL, backtracking until he came to the main road before turning once more toward O'Doud's mansion. Better he wasted a half-hour of his time than allow suspicion to fall on Ione Gilpatrick's head by following her too closely.

He whoaed his horse at the rail out front and dismounted, easing his bad leg to the ground. The yard was quiet. Even the old hostler remained out of sight. Osgood climbed the steps and lifted the brass rapper. Almost immediately the door opened, revealing Selah O'Doud in the opening. She wore a pink afternoon dress, fancy enough for a ladies' tea party in one of the big houses on San Francisco's Nob Hill. Sadly out of place in the Idaho woods, Osgood thought. And did she always wear that insipid color?

"My father isn't here," she said in answer to his query. "He had business in Eagle City today. May I give him a message?"

Osgood didn't think so. He didn't want to involve this innocent and rather vapid girl in her father's activities.

He shook his head. "It's nothing so important it can't wait. I'll talk to him later." He was startled when Jensen's thin face and narrow shoulders appeared behind Selah.

"Marshal?" Jensen said, taking charge. He glanced at his boss's daughter. "I'll handle this." It was a dismissal they all recognized.

Selah smiled as Osgood thanked her. Perhaps it was a courtesy she didn't often receive. But, although she wrinkled her nose at Jensen, she obeyed him unquestioningly and disappeared into the depths of the house. Jensen acted almost as though she were invisible. Osgood, guessing, had a hunch he'd been warned off the girl at some time or another.

"Back so soon, Osgood?" Jensen stepped outside and closed the door.

Osgood studied the man. Was the smirk lifting the corner of Jensen's mouth meant to be as derisory as it looked? "Thought Mayor O'Doud might want to know I was ambushed last night on my way home," he said. "Warn him to be on the lookout for any suspicious characters."

"Is that right?" Jensen was not a good enough actor. It was easy to see the news came as no surprise.

"That's right." Osgood decided it wouldn't hurt to stir the waters. "Believe I winged the culprit. He wasn't much of a shot."

Right on cue, Jensen's face darkened. "Could be you got lucky, Marshal."

"Could be." Osgood shrugged. "But he's the one lost blood, not me." If he hadn't been watching, he would've missed the way Jensen reached involuntarily toward his leg. "So I brought word," he continued. "I thought O'Doud ought to know."

Jensen's voice grated. "I'll tell him."

"Yeah. You do that."

Not making a show of it, but without turning his back, Osgood untied the horse and climbed aboard. Neither man had any more to say. He turned the gelding and headed back to town, the center of his back crawling until he was out of sight.

He had, Osgood believed, gotten answers to one or two questions, just now.

***

"I'LL BUY HIM," Osgood said, handing the brown gelding's reins to Leonard. He'd arrived back in town, well-satisfied with the horse, if with nothing else this day. It had moved well in the dark, sure-footed and unafraid, unlike some he had ridden. "Forty-five dollars including the gear. Will you board him for me?"

"I can do that." Leonard winked. "I'll give you a good price."

All the traffic would bear, Osgood figured. But the scoop of grain Leonard poured in the manger for the gelding was generous, and he was satisfied.

With the care of his horse seen to, Osgood stopped in at the jail, let the dog in, built up the fire, and headed down to Magda's for his own supper. Magda wasn't at work. Instead, there was a young girl waiting on tables. He must have made her nervous because she managed to spill gravy over the side of his plate, and coffee into his mashed spuds. He missed the older woman's cheery smile and practiced banter. Or maybe he was just bone-tired and cranky along with it.

Leaving the café, well-fed and in need of a full night of sleep, Osgood headed out on his final inspection of the town before turning in. He was starting down the street toward Bessinger's and the stage depot when a woman's pained scream, quickly stifled, grabbed his attention. The scream, plus loud, drunken laughter and the clatter of a tinny piano drew him towards the Chain and Choker Saloon. He figured somebody must be starting his Saturday night celebration a day early—and he didn't like the sound of it.

He'd been meaning to drop in at the local watering hole, he recollected. No time like the present.

The noise had come through the saloon door, which he found propped open by a filthy brass spittoon. The heavy wooden planking surprised Osgood, accustomed as he was to the light batwing doors at the entrance of such establishments further south. He was afraid it was an indication of the winter weather common hereabouts, and the storms that would soon sweep down on the mountain country.

He pushed through the gap. Immediately, everyone quit talking. The piano player came to the end of the song and ceased pounding the keys. The sudden silence made him grin. He guessed everybody knew who he was.

Discounting the people, the first thing he noticed was the flooring, thick as in any barn. Its most prominent features were the gouges and scars that disfigured the rough pine. Calked boots again, he supposed. He had yet to see a lumberjack in town who went without them. About midway into the room, five men were seated at one of the round tables. Each wore the spiked boots, heavy canvas jeans held up by suspenders, and bright flannel shirts with the sleeves rolled above the elbow. The smell of pitch clung to them, on their clothes, probably, overriding the stink of sweat. An improvement, Osgood thought.

There were other people in the room, but it was this group that held his attention because of the two women with them. The ladies didn't look happy, although one of them was trying hard. The brown-haired one had black-stained tear streaks running down her face. The screamer, he supposed, but if so, she didn't open her mouth and gripe to him. None of them said a word.

Osgood walked towards the bar. While his body was turned to the men, he made a point of slipping his holster loop from over the Smith & Wesson's hammer. The way the lumberjacks stared at the badge on his coat made it feel like a target. It would be a mistake to think that, because these men weren't cowboys, they didn't carry guns. They did. And knives, too. Under their shirts and in their boots, which were, he knew, weapons themselves.

"Gentleman," he said, halting beside the table. "In case you haven't heard, I'm TJ Osgood, the marshal of this fine city. I run a clean town. If you have any trouble, any disagreements with anybody while you're here, you come to me." He allowed his gaze to alight on the tear-stained woman a moment before it passed to the man who had an arm looped around her shoulders. His forearm bulged with taut muscle.

"It's my job to take care of fights," Osgood continued, briefly meeting the woman's eyes. "I don't allow them in my town. Likewise, I encourage you not to make trouble. Any townsman—or woman—comes to me with a complaint about you, I'll take care of that, too."

"Everytink she is yust fine here," the logger said, his handlebar mustache fluttering where it drooped over his mouth. Although not as tall as average, he was built big and burly. "Ain't it, boys? Ain't it, Sophie?"

The woman, clasped in an embrace that looked more captive than amorous, sniffed and nodded. A couple of the men grinned. The others hastened to add their assurances to the fineness of the situation.

"I'm glad to hear it. Enjoy yourselves." Osgood touched his hat. "Ladies."

Renewed silence escorted him to the bar, until the piano started up again. He bellied close to the smoothly adzed pine counter, propping his sore leg on the two-by-four foot rail. The Chain and Choker was not, he thought, what you'd call an elegant gentleman's club.

"I heard a scream," he said, ordering a short beer from the bartender.

"Sophie." The bartender moved uncomfortably. "She's all right."

"Is she? I'm glad to hear it. Not many folks out tonight. With all the commotion I heard from down the street, I expected more."

The bartender drew Osgood's beer and set it on the counter in front of him.

"This is quiet, compared to most times O'Doud's boys are in town. And they're here every Saturday night, along with the other crews. Town folk generally skedaddle when they show up." The bartender occupied himself by wiping the same glass over and over with a dirty towel, speaking from the side of his mouth, lips barely moving.

"Is that right?" Osgood sipped the sour beer, licking off the foam and grimacing. Beer had never been his tipple. "Why might that be, do you suppose?"

The bartender's jaw clamped shut, his eyes swiveling toward the table.

Another man, a slender, old feller in a worn black frock coat, stood at the bar close to Osgood. He smiled faintly as he took it upon himself to answer Osgood's question. "Could be because there's nothing O'Doud's men like more than a fight. And they always win."

"Always?" Osgood put a bit of skepticism in the question. "You mean they're that much tougher than other crews?"

"O'Doud hires the best and the toughest. It takes a strong crew of men just as good as they are to give 'em a whipping—

and, mister, that don't come about very often. Happens they got some advantages."

"Like what?"

"Like knowin' O'Doud will buy them out of jail. Meanwhile, the other fellers end up paying the doc to fix them up good enough they can go to work the next day so's they can pay the court costs. O'Doud's crew gets first chance at the girls, too—and they're hard on girls."

The bartender nodded. A shout from the table demanded another round of beer. He started drawing glasses full from the tap, taking his time at it. He motioned the woman who'd been weeping to come fetch them. "You all right, Sophie?" he asked.

Wearily, she shrugged. "I suppose. I been hurt before, and I expect I will be again."

"Do you want to bring charges?" Osgood couldn't help but notice the red mark on her cheek and another on her breast above the low neckline. They were already blotching purple.

Slowly, she shook her head, an almost imperceptible movement. "I don't want anybody getting killed on my account."

"You let me worry about that."

She met his eyes. "No, sir. Don't you see? That's what they want."

"To get me?" Osgood's expression didn't change. They might have been talking about the weather. "Me, specifically?"

Mutely, she bobbed her head once as she arranged the full glasses on her tray.

He took another sip of his beer. "They say why?"

"Yes, sir. Because you're pokin' around into that Gilpatrick boy's hangin'."

Osgood stilled, his eyes narrowing.

"They're the ones spoke against him," she explained softly. "Johansson, he said he's going to stop you from investigatin'. He's meanin' to stomp you. You better get out of here while you still can, Marshal. He's had a lot of beer. He's workin' himself up to a fight pretty fast."

There was a mirror over the back of the bar. A small plain one, not even painted with the requisite naked beauty, but in it he could see the burly lumberjack watching his every move.

"I appreciate the warning, Sophie," he said. "You know you're taking a chance on him hitting you again."

"Oh, Johansson wanted me to tell you. He wants you to worry some first, before he comes after you. His idea of a good time."

At this, Osgood's laughter boomed out, sounding hollow even to himself. "Me? Worry about him? Little lady, that's why I carry a gun."

The black-clad man beside him stirred. Osgood recognized the older man now. The same one he'd met over the outlaw he'd clubbed down with the hammer.

What had Tompko named him? Meredith.

"You carrying that hammer around with you, too, Mr. Osgood?" Meredith asked with a sly grin. He turned sober. "It'll be better than that pistol when you get in close with these boys. That's how they like to fight, you see. Up close. Gouging and scratching…that's their game. And they're good at it. I saw Johansson chew off a man's ear once. Don't you ever think they'll fight clean. They won't."

Osgood's smile was grim. "What makes you think I will?"

Chapter 9

OSGOOD NURSED HIS SHORT BEER until the foam collapsed. By then, one of the loggers at Johansson's table had pulled the prettier of the two women into a cleared space in the middle of the floor and, to a jangled tune from the piano, was dancing her around in dizzying circles. Another man had dashed outside holding his gut. Osgood guessed his belly was awash in beer or whiskey he couldn't wait to be rid of.

The others were involved in a card game as Sophie stood behind Johansson, looking on. Every now and then she glanced over at Osgood in a startled manner, from which he figured the men were discussing him. The group was not as raucous as earlier.

He couldn't help but catch the gleam as Johansson's eye periodically rested on him. If it was meant to unnerve him, it was working, although he kept his face impassive. Looked like the lumberjack had a plan in the works, and not one that boded well for him.

In view of the prostitute's warning, he had a notion this might be a good time to duck out of the Chain and Choker. If the loggers forced a fight on him, as the woman had implied they would, he didn't want to be forced into a corner. He preferred enough space around himself to maneuver—and fire his gun without breaking any mirrors or hitting any bystanders. And the fight would come to guns, he knew. He wasn't in any shape to duke it out, toe-to-toe.

Dropping a nickel on the counter, he left most of his beer in the glass and walked abruptly to the door. His bad leg ached under his weight, the muscles tight after a few hours in the saddle. Just as well he didn't plan on doing any running.

Outside, he heard the sick man heaving his belly dry in the alley alongside the saloon. From the noise, a man would believe the logger incapacitated. However, as Osgood had learned from previous experience, he couldn't depend on that being true. Some men could empty out and five minutes later be back getting a refill of popskull or what other poison he favored. For all he knew, this feller was one of those hardy souls.

Stepping silently around the man, Osgood captured the hand the drunk had braced against the saloon wall, jerked it backward and snapped one end of a pair of handcuffs around the wrist. He'd already spied a lightning rod running up the wall beside the brick fireplace. It took only a second to attach the loose end of the cuff to it.

"Hey!" the drunk yelped in belated protest. He peered around at Osgood out of reddened, hazy eyes. "Hey." He gave the cuff a vigorous yank, but the lightning rod, deeply planted in the ground, held firm.

"You're under arrest." Osgood said. "You'll be my guest in the jail overnight."

"Wha' for?"

"For being drunk, disorderly, and puking on a public street." Osgood ignored the fact they weren't, precisely, in the street.

The logger didn't notice the lapse. "You can't do that," he said. "The boys'll have me outta the jug in no time."

"I reckon they won't, mister, since they'll be right in there with you."

Osgood took his second set of manacles from his pocket and slipped the doubled cuff part over the fingers of his left hand. When his fingers closed on the underside, he had the outer rims as reinforcement to his bare knuckles. This done, he slid his revolver from the holster and stepped to the corner of the building.

He was barely fast enough in his preparations. Someone flung the saloon door wide, knocking the spittoon onto its side where it spilled its noxious load. The door crashed into the wall, and stuck there, light from interior spilling as far as the alley entrance. There was the sound of bodies crowding through a too-narrow opening.

The light threw tall, man-sized shadows to where Osgood stood in the dark alley. Hobnailed boots pounded and squeaked as they stuck in the boardwalk in front of the saloon, and then were pulled free. He listened, the low mutter of voices reaching him.

He should have gagged the sick man, he realized, when a shout rising from behind him gave his location away. Except he hadn't wanted the bugger strangling on his own vomit. Misplaced compassion because maybe, he thought now, that wouldn't have been such a bad idea.

Three of them came at him in a rush.

The first man to step around the corner went down like a puppet with his strings cut. Two quick, progressively harder taps on the noggin with the barrel of Osgood's pistol saw to that. Trouble was, it had taken too long. Both the other men jumped him before he could finagle himself some breathing space.

According to Sophie's warning, the two who grabbed for him were the worst of the bunch—two tough Scandinavian loggers with a reputation to maintain. Johansson's reputation preceded him, and the man Meredith had called Swede was noted for his delight in getting a man down, then stomping him with his spiked logging boots. Osgood was glad he'd taken the precaution of wrapping his fist in steel.

Lashing out with his left, Osgood chose Swede to catch the brunt of his attack. Blood spurted from Swede's lower lip, cut all the way through by Osgood's metal-clad hand. Grunting as he was caught unaware by the blow, Swede kept bulling in on Osgood, hardly deterred.

"He's mine," Swede said, sweeping Johansson out of his way.

Osgood's arm was jarred all the way to his shoulder, still tingling as he and Swede grappled. Swede punched low, aiming to damage Osgood's kidneys. The lumberjack landed a hit on the small of Osgood's back, connecting with the pocket gun the marshal kept there. He growled, both surprise and pain in the sound, giving Osgood the chance to retaliate with a couple of clips to the back of Swede's neck. The bigger man shook his head, dazed. But still he kept coming.

Hurt him, Osgood thought in satisfaction. But his mind was reeling from pain of his own. Swede's strike on the concealed pistol had hit a nerve, forcing his already weak leg to go numb. He was hardly sure if the leg was even capable of bearing him, and he leaned into Swede and let the other man's muscles take his weight. It was all that kept him upright as he beat at the same spot, over and over, on the logger's skull.

Sweat dripped from Osgood's face. His shirt was wet between the shoulder blades and he could hear himself breathing in whooping gasps after taking a series of punches to the belly. He had to end it fast, before the logger ended it for him, for he had no real stamina.

Swede continued, despite all of Osgood's efforts, to fight hard. The logger was confident, certain in his great physique, his strength, his years of no-holds-barred combat. It must have been this self-assurance that finally allowed Osgood to reach in over Swede's shoulder and chop down with all his strength between the logger's neck and shoulder blade. Swede's eyes suddenly rolled back in his head. He sank to his knees, and then sat, quiet as a kid on his first day of school. He wasn't knocked out, but merely rendered quiescent.

Osgood had no time to congratulate himself, or even catch his breath, before Johansson swarmed in to take the first man's place. He was as fast and angry as a bear smoked from its den.

Osgood staggered, overwhelmed by Johansson's aggression and the glancing blow delivered to his cheekbone. Half-stunned, the pistol flew from his hand. Johansson moved faster than he'd expected of the heavyset man. Knowing he must protect his vulnerable face and belly from the bigger man's battering, Osgood retreated a step. Stay out from under his boots. It was the only thought in his mind. Don't let him get you on the ground.

He swung his left fist, still wrapped in the metal cuff, but Johansson was ready, catching it in his calloused palm. Osgood's fingers were crushed against the steel as the logger squeezed, his grip as powerful as a blacksmith's vice. Aware that pulling away would only increase the pain, Osgood lunged forward, butting into Johansson's chin, and surprising him into letting go. But even as he felt the pressure release, Johansson's knee was smashing into his groin. Only the fact the blow was not delivered full on saved him.

Agony surged through him anyway. He twisted, falling to one knee. Air wheezed in his lungs, as if he'd forgotten how to breathe.

Johansson chuckled. "Stupid city marshal. Too weak for us boys from the woods, ja? If you done like da boss tells you, you don't get hurt." He laughed out loud. "Too late."

He hauled his foot back, the spikes gleaming like sharpened nails, and then kicked out at Osgood's head. At the last moment, Osgood saw it coming and dodged. He fell onto his side, taking a soft hit in the hip, instead of full force to the face. Agony blazed anew. But as he fell, he spied the Smith & Wesson lying only a foot away. Osgood was already moving. He kept going, squirming and stretching his full length for the pistol, even as the rest of him was left vulnerable to

Johansson's assault. And then his fingers closed on the familiar walnut grip. He yanked the pistol up level.

"Hold it." His voice was shaky. "We're done, friend, and you're under arrest."

Johansson had another of those belly laughs. "The boss, he don't pay me to stop a job before it's done."

His foot kicked out again, but he never delivered the blow. Osgood shot him in the knee, flesh and bone disappearing in a spray of gore that showered the saloon's outside wall.

Johansson bawled like a baby.

The single gunshot might as well have been an invitation to the party. A few brave folks came to investigate the noise, the first among them being Meredith, who cautiously peered around the corner of the saloon. Right behind him, the bartender held a lantern high overhead, illuminating Johansson writhing in a spreading puddle of blood.

"Well," Meredith said, sounding amazed. "To tell the truth, I expected to find something different out here. You're alive."

"I believe I am." Wishing that kick to the groin could be ignored, Osgood remained where he was—on the ground. Right at the present, he found the alternative to being alive just about as appealing. He shoved his pistol back in the holster.

"We gonna need the undertaker?" asked the bartender, peering at the man Osgood had pistol-whipped. He, alone of them all, wasn't moving.

"Better get Doc Worthy first," Osgood said. "I think Ritter is going to get the day off."

"I'll fetch the doc," a bystander said. They could hear his footsteps, running.

"Help me up," Osgood demanded.

It was the bartender, a more substantial man than the elderly Meredith, who reached down a hand and hoisted the marshal to his feet.

Osgood soon had Johansson disarmed, the lumberjack's hands manacled with his second set of cuffs. The cuffs were bent now, out of their perfect round, from the use they'd been put. Swede made no protest as he, too, was searched and his wrists tied behind him with a bit of rope the bartender produced.

Carrying Johansson and dragging the unconscious man between them, the whole bunch moved inside. There, they discovered the logger who'd been dancing with the saloon girl had vamoosed.

"He must've seen what happened to his friends." Meredith smirked. "Decided he didn't like the odds."

"He ran out the back like he smelled a skunk in here," the girl volunteered. She had a smile on her face.

"Just as well," Osgood said. "One less prisoner to worry about." Despite the confidence he portrayed, he felt a tad apprehensive since he expected the boss of the outfit, or whoever claimed responsibility for these yahoos, would soon have a full report of tonight's doings. What would be his next move? Another ambush? A shot in the back like happened to Blodgett?

Osgood was in no hurry to find out.

A few minutes later, Doc Worthy bustled in, his black bag bulging with medical instruments. He diagnosed two cracked heads. "Not serious," he assured the marshal. "A man's got to have a brain before it can be addled."

"I can interrogate them?" asked Osgood.

Worthy grinned. "For all the good it'll do." He looked with some glee upon Johansson's wound, pronouncing the necessity of taking the man to surgery, and commandeering a set of stretcher-bearers to carry him off.

"Don't worry," he told Osgood. "When I get through with him, he won't be going anywhere for a while. And added, at Osgood's question, "Laudanum. For heaven's sake, man. What did you think? That I was going to cut off his leg whether it needs it or not? That diagnosis remains to be seen." But he winked. "Speaking of laudanum, you look like you could use a dose yourself."

Osgood didn't say so out loud, but he felt like he could use a dose, too. He shook his head, smiling slightly. He hadn't known until then his lip was split and bleeding. Or that his eye was swelling until he could barely see out of that side.

With all the effort taken out of it, plenty of men were anxious to assist in hustling the prisoners over to the jail. Badger, woken out of a sound sleep by the flood of visitors, stood up and growled at the invasion, sensing which of the men were prisoners and which were not. Osgood was impressed.

"Down, boy," he said. The dog responded as though he'd been told, "Sic 'em," growling, and with his lips curled back over his fangs.

Osgood's helpers manhandled the most severely beaten man into the jail cell where they lay him on the bunk. He was followed in short order by the drunk. That left Swede, still groggy, tied to the office chair by the rope wrapped around his arms and legs. Osgood had been a lawman too many years to take a chance on a prisoner being quick enough to escape, no matter how whipped he appeared. Besides, he had a certain respect for the lumberjack's fists.

"What're you going to do with them?" Meredith hung around after the others finally left, having appointed himself the marshal's unofficial deputy in Tompko's absence.

Osgood went over to the water bucket and dipped out a ladle full. Before drinking, he rinsed his mouth and spat through the open door, tasting blood from his cut lip.

"I'm going to ask this feller a few questions," he said. "I'm going to ask him who his boss is, for starters. And who set this bunch on me."

Meredith feigned surprise. "Ask him? What for? You know who pays this crew's wages. O'Doud." He turned toward Swede, who sat with his eyes closed. "Ain't that right?"

Swede ignored the old man.

"Mr. Meredith," Osgood said, "this is my job. Maybe you'd better let me handle the questioning."

"What's your plan, Osgood? Beat the truth out of him?"

From Meredith's expression, the idea held appeal. Osgood couldn't help wondering what had stirred the burr in his britches. He smiled, wincing as his lip split a little farther. "I hope it doesn't come to that. What you could do, which would be a service to both me and the community, is have Dunfolk open up the telegraph office and send another message down to Coeur d'Alene City. Tell those deputies we got more prisoners that need picked up."

Meredith grinned. "They're going to think we got a regular den of iniquity up here, Marshal Osgood." He left, latching the door snugly behind him.

Osgood grunted. "More like a den of snakes."

At this, Swede rumbled into speech. "I ain't done nothin'. Yust drunk is all. Mr. O'Doud, he'll get us out of here before morning."

"Drunk?" Osgood forced a chuckle. "I'm afraid that isn't the charge against you, Swede. I'm holding you for attempted murder. Who told you to kill me?"

"Murder! The boss—" Swede stopped short, air whistling through his nose as he silenced himself.

"What about him?" Osgood urged. He bent near the man, almost whispering in his ear. "You're the one sitting in this chair, mister. You're the one who's going to hang. Remember the last hanging? Now we've got a precedent set. Where one hanging happens, another can follow. Gets easier every time."

Swede may not have scared easy, but it was clear he didn't like the sound of that. The chair Osgood had tied him to tilted and rocked as the logger struggled against his bonds, the legs bouncing on the floor. Osgood thought it was a good thing the chair was sturdily built. The prisoner only succeeded in giving himself rope burns.

Osgood soon discovered Swede had a bugle like a bull elk.

"You turn me loose," the logger yowled. "I ain't hanging for no murder. You ain't dead. The boss ain't goin' to like this."

Osgood had never felt more tired in his life. Not even when he'd been shot, awakening hours afterward shy a quart or so of blood. He sighed.

"I'm alive, all right, but not because you didn't try to kill me. You and your friends in there. All I have to prove is intention. I've got plenty of witnesses who'll swear that's what you meant to do. That's what you were ordered to do. Was it O'Doud did the ordering? Or maybe Jensen? Who?"

Swede only scowled.

"Tell me," Osgood said. "Otherwise—you hang. Just like Isaac Gilpatrick." Osgood exaggerated his case without compunction. The memory of Johansson's spiked boots aimed at his face would be with him a while.

"You yust wait," Swede yelped. "I ain't hanging."

Osgood shrugged and smiled, his lip oozing blood that he wiped away with the back of his hand.

"I ain't. Wait a minute."

Back in the jail cell, the drunk started a racket of his own. From the sound of things, he was trying to kick the door down. The dog whined, disturbed by the commotion.

"Swede," the drunk hollered, "you keep your trap shut."

"Gonna be some sight." Osgood lifted his voice for the men in the cell to hear. "The four of you—Johansson, he'll be on crutches—lined up on the gallows all at once. Unless they decide to take you one at a time. That'll work, too. Spread the fun, so to speak. Make it a real occasion."

Though his ruddy face paled, Swede took his compadre's advice to heart and shut his trap. Aside from a great many aches and pains, some of which were only now beginning to make themselves known, Osgood's fatigue kept him from caring all that much. Tomorrow would do as well, he decided. He'd separate the loggers and go at them one at a time.

Roughly, he jerked loose the knot he'd made in the bonds around Swede's feet, then went around to the back of the chair before releasing the one binding the man's shoulders. He left the prisoner's hands cuffed together.

"Get up," he said. "I'm sick of talking to you, and sick of your ugly face. Maybe by morning you'll see things a mite different. I want the name of the man who ordered me killed. That's it. Tell me that and, by gum, you never know but what I might go easier on you."

The logger blinked, but otherwise made no sign he'd heard.

Juggling the key to the cell door, Osgood gestured Swede to go ahead of him. They were right at the door between the holding cell and the office when his prisoner swept his booted foot toward Osgood's shin. Osgood leapt backward, reaching for his gun.

Swede, seeing his opportunity, put his head down and charged, slamming Osgood against the wall. Osgood grunted. Fresh pain radiated along battered nerves. He used the pistol barrel like a club, clouting Swede away. It was getting to be a routine.

"Get 'em, Badger," he yelled, hoping for a distraction. No one could have been more surprised than he when the dog bounded forward and sank his fangs deep into Swede's back pocket.

Swede belted out one whale of a yell. The distraction worked a charm.

"Well, I'll be a two-headed freak," Osgood muttered. Apparently, ole Badger had gotten a fair quantity of skin along with the pocket. It did Osgood's heart good.

With Osgood's pistol barrel jammed against his spine, and Badger still raring to take a bite out of his hind end, the logger calmed down fast. He allowed himself to be shoved into the cell with his friends.

"You'll see," he told Osgood, as though it were a threat. "We'll be outta here before morning. You wait and see. Boss'll take care of us."

Osgood banged the door shut on the crew, flipped the latch and locked it up tight as a drum. After that, it was about all he could do to make into the other room, where he sank down into the rocker and closed his eyes. The room whirled around and around like he was rolling downhill in a barrel.

Badger, back to his usual sleepy, placid self, sat between Osgood and the warm stove. He laid his head on Osgood's knee.

"You're a real wonder, Badger." Osgood rested his hand on the animal's head. Admiration—and gratitude filled him. "As good as an extra deputy any day. I wonder, did somebody teach you that, or are you a natural?"

Badger just sighed companionably.

Chapter 10

OSGOOD SAT ROCKING gently back and forth, too exhausted to stir, and wondering if Mrs. Gilpatrick—Ione— might be over at his cabin with something new to tell him. She had a knack of somehow gaining entry through the locked door slick as any wraith. If she sneaked in tonight, she'd have a long wait, unless, although it was dangerous, she dared come over here looking for him. He'd be spending the next few hours in the office, guarding his prisoners.

Pain washed over him. His bones and muscles ached, burning with an intensity that gained momentum with each tick of the clock. Cuts, bruises, and overstrained muscles craved immediate attention. Ignore it, he told himself, and like his mother always said, maybe it'll go away. The advice was easier given than followed.

Age must be creeping up on him because, as much as he hated to admit it, the fight tonight had been all he could handle. He was certain there'd be blood when he voided in the morning, the way his kidneys were burning. His bad leg ached; Johansson's spikes had left holes in his hip where spots of blood stained his britches, and the fingers the logger had crushed were already so swollen they looked like sausage links.

He flexed them, a test that proved they were about as responsive as those same fat sausages. What he longed for more than anything was a double shot of ole John Barleycorn—for medicinal purposes, of course, to help dull the pain. But no. He'd put that behind him. Osgood versus Whiskey was a fight he'd already won.

Pushing the rocker runners forward, he tipped himself out of the chair. Before he got too comfortable, he'd best build up the fire and fill the coffee pot. Which he did, spooning in a double portion of grounds. He'd need something strong, he figured, to get him through the night. If, as Swede expected, someone came to town with the intention of breaking the crew of loggers out of jail, the town marshal had better be awake and ready to defend himself.

He poured cold water into the washbasin, where he rinsed a fresh batch of blood from his cheekbone and cut lip. An errant thought came to him. If he had a woman—a wife—this would be her job. Succoring her returning warrior, keeper of the peace. Kiss away the pain. Osgood snorted. Some of the blows he'd taken must've made pudding of his brain. Now he was getting fanciful. Returning to his chair, he settled in for the night, coffee cup—and gun—handy.

He believed there'd be time to rest his eyes. Dawn was when trouble would come. If it came.

But if he did have such a woman, his thoughts drifted on, what would she look like? Tall, statuesque, with blue eyes? Or would she be small, dark and feisty? Before he could figure it out, his eyes closed.

***

OSGOOD JERKED AWAKE. His neck felt as if it were going to part company with his head, and he groaned, massaging the point of worst tightness until the muscles eased. During the night, as he found when he scrubbed hands over his face, the cuts had scabbed over, although they'd be easy to dislodge. Fresh pain brought him completely awake.

Although he felt stuck to the rocker, he forced his legs to support him once he was up and moving. The room had grown chill. Across the hall in the jail, he heard snores in at least two different, rather unmusical, octaves, loud as locomotives blowing off steam. Made him wonder how he had ever slept through it. A bigger wonder was how any of the cellmates had.

The stove clattered as he threw in a fresh chunk of wood. Badger whined to be let out into the growing dawn.

Dawn. The peace unbroken. The town of Black Crossing was silent when he opened the door and looked up and down the street. He hardly dared let himself feel relief. No sign of trouble disturbed the early quiet. Swede was apt to be mighty disappointed in his employer, he reflected.

Over at the livery, a lantern flared as Harvey Leonard came in early to start shoveling out stalls. At Magda's café, where a wisp of smoke from the cook fire was already making a darker smudge in the dark sky, folks were stirring around. Osgood's stomach rumbled. Here was a problem he hadn't foreseen. With a cell full of prisoners, he needed a deputy. With Tompko gone, who could he trust to watch the jail while he ate? Who could he send to fetch the prisoners' breakfast?

These questions were answered an hour later when Mr. Meredith turned up outside the office door. With him was Will Dunfolk, who carried a yellow telegraph flimsy in his hand. Osgood unlocked the door and let them in. It was broad daylight now, any attempt of a jailbreak likely over.

"Sheriff of Kootenai County is mighty impressed with you, Mr. Osgood," Dunfolk said. He sounded almost jovial.

"With me?"

"Yes, with you. Here's his telegram. Read it."

Sourly, Osgood took the paper, eyeing the pair of older men. "Everybody in town already know what it says, Mr. Dunfolk? Except for me?"

Dunfolk hung his head, but Osgood's comment didn't faze Meredith a bit. "If it had been a letter firing you, Marshal, we would've torn it up."

Osgood grunted and looked down at his message. Will take delivery of prisoners today—Stop—Filling up my jail—Stop—No more room—Stop "Guess this means Tompko got there with the outlaws all right." He read the short missive again before frowning. "Says today. Soonest he can get here is tomorrow, isn't it?"

Dunfolk answered. "He'll take the General Sherman up to Harrison Landing and cut on over by road. Be here in no time."

"General Sherman?"

"Lake steamer," Meredith explained. "Out of Coeur d'Alene City. Makes a run from there to Harrison Landing and on up to Cataldo Mission, hauling supplies bound for the mines. Takes on passengers, too."

"Well," Osgood said, "it'll suit me to see the last of these boys. Do you suppose, Mr. Dunfolk, I could bother you to have the café send over four breakfasts soon as it's convenient?"

Dunfolk glanced at him, eyes narrowing. "Certainly. Be glad to. Or maybe I can do even better by you." He rubbed the ribs Meredith was jamming with a bony elbow. "After seeing you fight last night, Meredith is champing at the bit to do his civic duty. Wants to be a hero. He's rarin' to stay here and keep an eye on your prisoners whilst you clean up."

"That right, Mr. Meredith?" Osgood was surprised by the gratitude he felt.

Meredith shoved his coat aside and stuck his thumbs between his armpits and his suspenders. "Hero. Hah! Dunfolk's getting carried away, Marshal. But I don't mind helping out. If you'll pardon my saying so, you don't appear any too spry."

The observation startled a growl out of Osgood. Spry? He'd bet he felt older all by himself than these two duffers' ages combined. "Tell you what," he said slowly. "Come back

126

8,000,000

90

$$9\,13 \overline{)9,300,000}$$

$$9\,3\,0\,9$$
$$9\,3\,0\,9$$
$$9\,0\,9$$
$$90$$

930,000,000

Lexington Public Library

www.lexpublib.org
(859) 231-5500

Number of items:

1

Barcode:0000223113788
Title:Cost of a killing the life and times of
Jeston Nash /
Due:9/4/2019

8/7/2019   10:37 AM

in an hour, Mr. Meredith. If everything is peaceful, I'll hold you to it."

Meredith grinned, blithe as a new groom. "Well, of course it'll be peaceful. Why wouldn't it? You've got three of the worst hard cases in this country in jail, with the big bull of the woods laid up over at Doc's place."

Osgood shook his head. "Johansson isn't the one giving the orders. Swede says he expects his boss to get him out, and I don't think he was talking bail. Whoever it is, he'll be the big bull."

"Who..." A startled expression passed over Meredith's face. "You mean...O'Doud?"

"Swede isn't saying." Osgood shrugged. "Frankly, I wouldn't have been surprised if a mob had showed up earlier. Now I think the danger has passed, but you still might want to renege on your offer of help."

Looking worried at Osgood's warning, Dunfolk frowned, but Meredith wasn't bothered. "O'Doud is more apt to buy his men out of jail than break them out. He considers this his town. Besides, he hired you. You've only been here three days. Why would he want to get rid of you?"

"Didn't you hear that girl?" Osgood grimaced. "The reason they were after me is because I've been asking questions about Isaac Gilpatrick's hanging. And about Marshall Blodgett's murder."

"Blodgett?" Meredith's mouth pursed into a thin line. "I'll bring my Colt."

Osgood's visitors left then, Dunfolk to tend his business and Meredith, in his capacity as temporary deputy, to organize breakfast for the prisoners. This left Osgood with a few minutes of slack time. Might as well put those minutes to use, he decided. Moving stiffly, he called Badger over and led the dog back to the holding cell with him, calling out one prisoner's name. The man who'd been heaving his guts out in the alley appeared at the small, barred aperture in the plank door.

"You're McCammon?"

"That's me."

Osgood readied the handcuffs. "Hold both your hands in between the bars," he said. "When I have the cuffs on, I'll unlock this door and let you out. Rest of you stay where you are."

There was a subdued protest, muffled like a growling cat. Osgood heard someone, probably Swede whisper, "Yust keep your mouth shut, McCammon, and da boss'll take care of us."

"Yeah, yeah," McCammon whispered back. He thrust his hands through the bars. "I'm ready. Open the door."

Osgood drew his pistol. Using only one hand, he fumbled the cuffs into place over McCammon's thick wrists before stepping aside and turning the key in the lock. "All right. Come out." ·

He was almost disappointed when the other two didn't try to rush him. He reckoned Badger sitting on his haunches, waiting for a little sport, had a cooling effect on their dispositions. After what the dog had done to Swede last night, no one was eager to try his temper. They might've been afraid the dog would go after their front parts instead of their backsides.

McCammon blinked upon entering the office. Sunlight filled the main room with dazzling brightness after the dim light in the windowless cell. There was longing in his expression as he sniffed the air. "I'd take some of that coffee you've got brewing, and drink a dipper of water, too."

Osgood motioned him into the chair. "Later. There are a few questions I want answered first."

He didn't expect to learn much from McCammon, which kept him from being disappointed. Johansson was the one, Mac told Osgood, who'd instigated the attack on him, although all of them had been willing participants in the plot.

"Ain't nobody says Johansson is a liar and gets by with it," he said. He crossed his legs and rocked the chair back on its legs. "Call him a liar and you're callin' Swede and me and the other fellers liars, too. Reckon we don't stand for it neither."

"Truth rubs, eh?"

McCammon's face went crimson. He started to rise, the chair clattering onto all four legs.

His expression hard as the steel in his pistol, Osgood poked the barrel in the lumberjack's

chest and pushed him down again.

"We both know Johansson didn't order me beaten. Who did?" he demanded.

"Don't know what you're talkin' about." McCammon sneered. "Anytime I got a chance to stomp the marshal of a two-bit town like this one, I'll do it. Best fun in the world— besides having a woman."

Osgood straightened. "Tell me, McCammon, does it generally take four of you wood choppers to take a man down?"

McCammon's reply wasn't pretty, but it was in line with the other prisoners' reaction when Osgood put the same question to them. Marshal stomping, according to what they all said, was a favored form of entertainment.

"Along with shooting them in the back?" Osgood put the question to Swede when it was his turn.

"No guns. I use my fists, my feet," said Swede, and oddly enough, Osgood believed him. So maybe it hadn't been the loggers who'd murdered Marshall Blodgett. And maybe it hadn't been their boss. They knew who did, though, he was certain of that. It was someone who liked to use a gun. A name came to mind.

***

THE CREW'S BOSS came for them just as Osgood sat down to his breakfast. The men were silent in the cell, too involved in plowing their way through bacon, cackleberries and flapjacks, to notice as the marshal closed the door between the cellblock hallway and the main office.

Osgood reseated himself at the desk and reluctantly pushed his plate aside. He'd barely had time for a taste of Magda's good cooking.

"Mr. O'Doud," he said. "Mr. Jensen. Your crew said you'd be here. What can I do for you?"

O'Doud smiled as genially as though his last words to the marshal hadn't been a threat. "You can turn my boys loose, for starters, Mr. Osgood. This is a workday. I need them on the job. Swede sets choker, Johansson is crew boss."

Jensen said nothing, although he eyed Osgood's battered face with scarcely hidden glee. His step had seemed halting when he followed his boss in, although since he stood in back of O'Doud, it was hard to tell.

"I'm sorry to put you out," Osgood said, "but I'm afraid I can't turn them loose, Mayor."

O'Doud chuckled. "I'm sure you can't—until I pay their fines. How much, Mr. Osgood? And what about damages? They've been known to break out a window or two, or even smash a few chairs. All in good fun, of course. I ought to own the Chain and Choker by now, I've paid for so much glass."

He already owned the building, if Osgood correctly recalled something Benny had said. Only the saloon's liquor stock belonged to the occupant.

"If there are any damages to the saloon, you can settle up with the proprietor." Osgood paused. "As far as fines for your men go, those haven't been set. Your crew will be taken to Coeur d'Alene City later today and jailed until they come before the judge."

Red washed into O'Doud's heavily jowled face. "What are you talking about? Jailed over a simple fight? I believe you're overstepping your bounds, Osgood."

Osgood scooted his chair away from the confines of the desk. "Bounds overstepped, weren't overstepped by me. Your crew went too far, when they took me on. Assaulting an officer of the law carries a few more penalties than laying into the drunk standing next to them at the bar."

Feigned surprise arched O'Doud's brows. "You mean, they picked on you? Why? Were you the drunk standing next to them, Marshal?"

A butterfly landing on a rosebud would have sounded loud in the silence that followed.

Once, Osgood conceded, O'Doud's accusation might have been true. But no more, and never again. Odd, the way the mayor kept bringing that part of his past up. To what purpose?

His chair scraping across the floor, Osgood stood up, carefully keeping his expression bland. "Makes me wonder why you want these men running wild in the town you claim is yours, Mr. O'Doud. And as much as I'd like to accommodate you, I'm afraid you'll have to ride over to Coeur d'Alene City to buy these boys out of jail. I doubt court will be in session over there until Monday. Looks like your crew is taking a little vacation."

O'Doud's glare was enough to have struck as lesser man dead. "You're forgetting something, Osgood. I hired you, and I can fire you. Which I'm doing right now."

"No, sir. I'm afraid you can't fire me. Best read the contract we both signed. Judge Doerner swore me in, and it'll take a vote of the city council to get rid of me. And I've got to tell you, Mayor, that the only man mad at me around here is you."

"For now, maybe. But be careful who you antagonize, Osgood." The mayor was pale in his anger. "I hope you're not forgetting what happened to Marshal Blodgett."

"No, sir." Osgood's eyes locked with O'Doud's. "I'm not forgetting."

Half-hidden by O'Doud's bulk, Jensen stirred. Osgood's hand rested on the butt of his gun, already loose in the holster.

Meredith, coming back for his stint of watching the prisoners, stood aside as first O'Doud, then Jensen, pushed unceremoniously out the door. Jensen came close to knocking the older man down, deliberately setting his hand against Meredith's chest and shoving.

"Who pissed on their campfire?" Meredith asked, picking a splinter out of the hand he'd slapped against the wall to keep from being bowled over.

Osgood stuck the tine of his fork into his congealed eggs. He'd lost his appetite, but he raised a grin at the question. "Reckon I did. Mr. O'Doud seemed to think his say-so was enough to get his men out of jail. I told him it wasn't. So then he tried to fire me. You all right?"

Meredith shrugged and blew a sound that was a cross between a baby's slobber and a horse neighing. "Mr. Osgood, you've either got more guts than a Polish sausage maker, or you aren't too bright. Have you forgotten what happened to your predecessor?"

Osgood figured of the two choices Meredith posed, he probably qualified for the second. Aloud, he said, "Funny. That's just what O'Doud asked me."

While breakfast no longer appealed to Osgood, Badger had no such prejudice against cold eggs and soggy pancakes. He sucked the food into his gullet like he hadn't had a bite for a week and stood whipping his tail against Osgood's legs, staring up at the man with soulful brown eyes as if to beg for more.

Meredith tut-tutted at the waste of good food and shooed the animal outside.

Black Crossing was a strange place, Osgood decided. They'd hired sight unseen, except for O'Doud, a broke-down feller whose past included a problem resisting liquor. Then they put him in charge of law enforcement with only the inexpert help of one underage deputy, a hound dog, and the volunteer services of a retired businessman. These few, to contend with timber jumpers and murderers. A perfect set-up if you wanted it to fail—perfect for the timber jumpers and murderers, at least. They couldn't have done better if they'd tried.

And, as Benny Tompko had told him, and as Ione Gilpatrick had tried to convince him, and as everybody else in town had hinted at, just maybe they had tried.

Osgood shook his head in wonder. He hadn't wanted to believe it, but unless he was mistaken, O'Doud was barely bothering to hide his criminal activities.

"I don't think you have anything to worry about, Mr. Meredith, in watching the prisoners. Not anymore. If you're all set, I'm going over to the cabin and change my shirt." He was sick of the bloodstains down the front, plus, although hidden by his jacket, all of one armhole had torn out and grown uncomfortable.

"Go ahead. Go. Take your time, Marshal. I'm good." The old man waggled his Peacemaker as proof he was ready for any desperadoes who might come his way.

What he needed most, Osgood reflected as he limped along the path towards his cabin, was a hot bath and a goodly dose of paregoric to ease his aches and pains. He wanted to see if he truly did have holes in his hip from Johansson's spikes, or if the sensation was only the prick of his imagination. Most of all, he wanted to sleep for about ten hours.

With his mind on his various injuries, at first he missed the item that clamored for his attention. His cabin door stood wide open, he saw now, the interior eerily dark in contrast with the bright morning, yet he distinctly remembered locking up. Drawing his pistol, he slowed, watching for an ambush. Fallen pine needles muffled his footsteps on the path. Walking lightly, he stepped up onto the porch step, only to have it creak beneath his weight with a sound loud as a pistol shot—or so it seemed. Lurching forward, he sprang to the opening and ducked within, back to the wall.

"Hold it right there," he ordered, pointing his.44 at the intruder.

At the same time, he heard a startled gasp and the figure seated at his table spun to face him.

"TJ! Marshal Osgood...where have you been? I've got something to tell you."

Chapter 11

HE MIGHT'VE KNOWN it would be her. Even though she was taking an awful chance, showing up here in daylight.

Tension shivered along Osgood's nerves, a tension the excitement—no, impatience—in Ione Gilpatrick's voice did nothing to dispel. If anything, it grew worse. He'd dreamed of her being here, in his cabin, last night. In his dream, she'd been wearing a blue dress. And here she was, only in life she had on a plain brown skirt and a yellow blouse. A man's belt cinched her slim waist. She'd called him TJ.

"Ma'am," he said, sheathing his pistol yet another time. "Ione. How'd you get in here?" He entered, closing the door on the glare of sunlight.

"The key." She rose, standing quietly as he stalked toward her. "I noticed where you put it when I was here before. I hope you don't mind."

Did he? He thought maybe he did, if only because he felt like a fool, bursting in the way he had and letting her get under his skin. But he couldn't tell her that and remained silent as he peeled out of his jacket. Drawing the short-barreled Remington from behind his back, he set it on the table. Immediately, his hip felt a touch better.

"You are angry," she said, reading his expression with unerring accuracy. "I'm sorry. I shouldn't have come."

"What did you have to tell me?"

"I...I..." She studied him, apparently losing track of what she was saying as she eyed the bloody rags of his shirt. Perhaps his face, which he supposed had turned all the colors found in nature by now, startled her also.

"What happened?" Her voice rose. "Who did this to you? Was it O'Doud? Or Jensen?"

Osgood snorted. "The day Colin O'Doud can do this to me is the day I turn in the badge."

"Oh. I thought—"

"It was his men, all right. His logging crew." Osgood interrupted her, whatever she'd thought. "But they aren't mentioning their boss by name."

She shuddered. "Another ambush?"

Smiling wryly, he found his valise, still packed with the things he'd brought with him on the stage, and dug out a clean shirt. "You could say so, I suppose," he admitted, shaking a few wrinkles from the cotton. "One I walked into of my own accord."

"Why?"

"Why? Because I hired on to keep the peace in Black Crossing. That's what folks are paying me for, and that's what I intend to do."

She shook her head. "How badly are you hurt?" She answered her own question. "Badly enough to make mush of your brains, it looks like. They'll keep after you, TJ, until something tips them over the edge and they kill you. I know they will. This is a pattern, like what they did to Marshal Blodgett and what they did to Isaac."

For the first time within the last twelve hours, Osgood experienced a burst of well-being. The smile he flashed at her felt like it hadn't been used in ten years or so. And maybe it hadn't.

"I thank you for your concern, Ione." His use of her name was deliberate. "But maybe you ought to be asking how they feel."

"Pardon me?"

His grin widened, until he felt his split lip crack and began to seep again. It didn't matter. "I won this round. The men responsible are in my holding cell waiting for transport over to the Coeur d'Alene City jail. And Colin O'Doud, I'm sorry to say, is spittin' mad."

"In your holding cell?" She repeated his words. "His men are in jail? You mean…"

"I mean some of those fellers look worse than I do. If that's possible."

His words must have struck a chord in her, for Ione walked over to him and peered into his face. She reached up, fingertips barely grazing the gash Swede had opened above his eyebrow.

"Sit down," she said, as if he were a wayward student. "Those cuts need tended."

She saw to lighting the stove herself, likewise drawing water and heating it. He needed his rest, she said, her mission changed, for the moment, to ministering to his needs. Once she asked if he'd ever been married, a curiously personal question from a woman he judged naturally reticent.

"No," he said, and added deliberately, "not yet."

The scene was nearly the same as he'd imagined as he'd dozed away the hours of the long night. Except her hands were surer and gentler than the ones in his dream, and with her standing above him as she washed his wounds, he could smell her scent. Something spicy, like cloves and sweet grass.

All of which didn't mean her ministrations outside the dream were painless. To the contrary. She found sore spots he hadn't known he possessed, including a knot on his head. He tried not to let her see how pain zinged along his nerves, or to show his awareness in being this close to her. In truth, he tried to put what he felt down to his being without a woman for a long, long time.

Too long. "Must be it," he muttered to himself.

"What did you say?" Her storm dark eyes peered into his.

Considering the line his thoughts had been running, Osgood couldn't help but be embarrassed. He'd just been thinking the touch of her lips might well have made him feel better. "You said you had something to tell me," he said.

She paused in dabbing at the cut above his eyebrow. "Yes. All this clean put it out of my mind. I've found where O'Doud's men have been cutting timber on land he doesn't own."

"Timber jumping?"

Ione nodded, her expression fierce. "The crime of which they accused my son."

When she would have resumed her attempts at cleaning him up, Osgood caught her wrist, stilling her hand. "How do you know it's O'Doud's men?"

"Because early this morning I followed Mr. Jensen out to where a crew has been working. Oh, don't worry. He didn't see me. And no one was there."

Although there was triumph in her tone, Osgood's blood ran cold. "Ma'am," he said, his temper flaring, "I'm beginning to think you're the one isn't too bright. What if they'd caught you? You got any idea what they might've done? It's a lucky thing I've got the best part of his crew in jail."

She stiffened, rigid as a metal pipe and, as if it were contaminated, dropped the handkerchief she'd been using on his face into the basin of pink-tinted water. Osgood regretted his words, not for thinking them, but for saying them like that. She was offended, and no wonder.

"I'll have you know—" she began, but he cut her off before she could get into full swing.

"Last night," he said, "one of those men I arrested was in the saloon with a woman. He hit her, Ione, with no more thought than a man would cuff a disobedient dog. Hit her in the face hard enough to leave a bruise. If he felt free to mistreat a saloon girl right out in the open, what makes you think he'd hold off on hurting you when there's no one around to see? Maybe not just slapping you around, but worse."

He meant to scare her, and he succeeded. He could tell that much. But it only firmed her delicate jaw until she looked like a pugnacious bulldog. Growled like one, too.

"Are you interested in seeing what I've found, Marshal Osgood?" she asked, as if his concern was of no consequence. "After all, with those hooligans in jail, what danger can there be?"

He guessed he'd been put in his place. She was back to calling him Marshal Osgood. "I've got four men in custody," he said. "And I can tell you right now, none of them are Jensen."

"I have a shotgun," she declared. "I can take care of myself."

His voice softened. "Just point me in the right direction, Ione. As soon as my prisoners are picked up, I'll take a ride out to where they're working and see for myself. But I can't leave them to Mr. Meredith."

"You'll never find the way unless I show you," she said. "I wouldn't want you getting lost, you being new here and all."

He had a notion that was supposed to be an insult, payback on the one he'd given her. Well, she hadn't struck deeply enough. It was difficult, holding his laugh inside. And then seriousness hit again. "You said you carry a gun. Are you prepared to shoot a man with it? Shoot him dead?"

If she answered, he didn't hear, seeing a sudden, hearty pounding on his door silenced them both. Motioning Ione into a corner where she couldn't be seen, Osgood opened the cabin door a crack

"'Mornin', Mr. Osgood." It was Tompko, bright-eyed and bushy-tailed as a healthy young tree squirrel.

Osgood slapped him with a jaundiced eye. "What're you doing here? You put wings on that horse of yours?"

"No, sir." Overlooking the fact Osgood hadn't invited him in, Benny ducked under his boss's arm and entered the cabin.

"Me and my horse boarded the steamer early this morning—well, the middle of the night, I guess—and I rode up from the landing. You ever been on a steamer, Marshal? Shoreline sure is pretty from out on the lake. Makes me wish I could swim more than two arm flops."

As the deputy turned to face Osgood, his fair skin flamed. It was clear he'd caught sight of Ione Gilpatrick and written his own story as to what she was doing there. Especially in view of Osgood's dishabille.

"Benny," Ione said, coming forward, "I'm glad you're back. There you are, Mr. Osgood. You can leave those prisoners in Benny's capable hands and come with me right now."

"Prisoners? Somebody try to pull another robbery? Go with you where?" Benny spun back to the marshal, and finally got a good look at his face and the leftovers of Ione's care. "Holy smoke, Marshal! What happened to you?"

Osgood didn't feel up to answering that many questions all at once. Even if he could remember them all. "Assault," he said, thinking to save further explanation until later. What seemed important now, in view of Ione's insistence, was that his deputy take over the responsibility of the prisoners. He capitulated. She was right. Everything else could wait. He launched into the story of last night's events, keeping the telling short and terse.

"Here's what I want you to do," he finished up. "Johansson is over at Doc Worthy's surgery, taking up bed space. Doc said he'd keep him doped until he could be moved, so he won't get away. Soon as those other fellers are gone, you go on over and watch him. And I mean watch him. He's a tough bugger. You might be surprised at what he can do if he sets his mind to it."

Tompko was gawking at him all bug-eyed, causing Osgood to wonder if the deputy had heard a word he'd said.

"You took 'em all on? By yourself? And won?"

Benny didn't need to sound so incredulous, Osgood thought sourly. "I'll give you some advice, Tompko," he said.

"If you get in a tight spot, don't be afraid to assert yourself. More lawmen been killed by hesitating than by taking the initiative."

"Yes, sir."

"Scoot on over to the jail now, Benny, and relieve Mr. Meredith. You know what to do until I return."

"You bet." Tompko started out the door, pausing on the threshold. "You be careful, Marshal. Remember, Sheriff Blodgett was murdered when he rode into the woods by himself."

"He won't be by himself," Ione said, her jaw set. "I'm going with him."

***

A QUARTER HOUR LATER, they were headed northeast, following the road away from town. Before long, they found an overgrown cut-off and turned onto it, heading deeper into the forest. Ione told him this was an old logging road, and that they should be safe from prying eyes in case anyone—and here Osgood understood her to mean O'Doud—should decide to keep watch on the marshal.

"I believe O'Doud has other things on his mind right now," he said. "Such as rounding up another crew of men. Maybe hiring an attorney for the men in jail. He's bound to be shorthanded after last night."

"He pays his help well," she replied, a touch of bitterness in her tone. "Three or four men won't be hard for him to replace. More men willing to do anything he tells them. There's plenty around who don't care what the job is, as long as there's money in it."

"There's truth in that," he agreed. "But it'll take a while for the word to get out he's hiring."

The countryside they rode through was quiet. They saw no one. It was a warm day for October, with just enough breeze to set the tree tops whispering. Ione wore only a tan, cable knit sweater over her yellow blouse.

Osgood couldn't help noticing she sat her sidesaddle well, and that the little piebald mare she rode was a dandy mover, even though knock-kneed and ugly as a mud hole in the snow. She'd left the mare tethered in the woods beyond his cabin, meeting him out on the road after he retrieved his horse from the livery and, as far as most anyone would be willing to swear, ridden out by himself.

"We shouldn't meet anyone else using this trail," she said, anchoring a gray hat on her head with a chin strap as their pace quickened. "Isaac showed it to me once." Her already husky voice choked in saying her son's name. "H...he said the only place it goes is down to the river from Mr. Finley's place. Mr. Finley used to dump logs in at a landing there and float them down to the sawmill at Harrison."

"Used to?" Osgood kept his eyes moving from the trail to the surrounding woods and even to the deep blue autumn sky. He hurt—and he was tired. Easy to miss what might be right under his nose.

"Yes," Ione said, regaining his attention. "He was hurt in a logging accident—he lost a leg to an infected axe cut—so he hasn't been out here for some time."

"Is that right?" Osgood's gaze sharpened. "Somebody has. Several somebodies, I'd say, from this mess of tracks. Look around you."

"Oh!" She peered down at the trail beneath her horse's feet and he watched realization dawn on her. "Can you tell how many?"

At her insistence, he give her a lesson in tracking, pointing out the broken limbs on the trees and bushes, the ground cut to pieces from sharp-shod animals, the fresh piles of horse manure, a cigar butt.

Ah, yes. A cigar butt of the same expensive brand Colin O'Doud had offered his guest.

142

"It doesn't look like they've been skidding logs through here," he said, filing the information in his mind. "Looks more like someone is using it for a way from here to there."

"I should've seen as much for myself." She sounded disgusted that she'd missed the obvious.

"How far until we're on this Finley feller's land?" Osgood asked.

"According to what Isaac told me, we're on it now. It runs from the river all the way to the other side of the Coeur d' Alene-Wallace road."

An impressive stand of mast-straight ponderosa pine lined both sides of the track. A scent of cedar also wafted down to them, with a perfume like fine wine. Osgood had to laugh at himself at the idea. Being with Ione Gilpatrick made him fanciful. He reckoned it must have rubbed off on him from her, although he allowed she hadn't said anything as silly at that to him. If only she weren't quite so foolhardy in her pursuit of the facts regarding her son's execution. He surely did hope, when they came to the end of all this, she wasn't disappointed with the conclusion.

Abruptly, the track ended in a clearing where even an old Pinkerton detective like him could tell the downed timber was fresh-cut. The smells of pitch and turpentine hung in the air. There were no logs in sight, but there were tall piles of slash full of unwilted greenery hauled to the side of the road. Stump wounds oozed beads of sap thick as clotted blood.

This may have been an illegal operation, but as far as he was concerned, it could've belonged to anybody. There wasn't a soul around; no one on which to fix the blame—if blame should be fixed at all.

"Could be Finley has hired himself a crew," he said, pointing out the obvious to Ione, but she disagreed.

"Finley's landing is back the other way. See here, Marshal Osgood, the skid marks from the logs that have been cut?" She had the hang of this tracking business now, and was showing him places where the forest floor was as deeply gouged as though it had been plowed, the grass and small bushes ripped from the earth. "As inexperienced as I am, it's impossible to miss seeing the direction they're going. Straight towards Colin O'Doud's land on the other side of the road. All we have to do is follow these signs to the finish, and we'll have the proof we need. We'll know once and for all whose outfit is logging off these trees. We'll know who the real timber jumper is."

"I'll follow the signs," he corrected. "It's time you went home."

"Home?" she echoed. "I will not. I'm seeing this through, no matter what happens. I want to be there when the man who killed my son gets what's coming to him."

"You've shown me the evidence—if evidence it is. I'll take it from here."

She reined her horse to a stop and frowned at him. "You are going to arrest him, aren't you?"

At this, Osgood sighed, certain his next words might well light a match under her. But he couldn't lie to her regarding what he was going to do, although he wished he could. He had a notion he'd be getting a firsthand look at the temper he'd been hearing about.

"An important man like Colin O'Doud, mayor of Black Crossing? Ione, I can't arrest a man, any man, based on what we've seen here today. And even if I follow the trail and find a pile of logs cut from Finley land sitting on O'Doud land, I'll still need to talk to Finley first. How do we know he hasn't sold his land or his timber?"

"Oh…but…"

"This looks suspicious. I'll be the first to agree with that, and I'm going to dig for facts, but the truth is, right this minute I don't have anything to arrest O'Doud for. There's nobody who's complained about their timber being stolen. Nobody who flat out said he ordered them to cut another man's timber. Nobody who flat out said he ordered the attack on me."

"Dig for facts," she said, as though that's all she'd heard. Her expression hardened, so that, for a moment she looked every one of her thirty-five years plus a few. "You do believe he's a crook, don't you? And a murderer?"

Osgood, thinking back to that ill-fated dinner he'd been invited to, and O'Doud's hinted threats, said, "Well, yes. I do. A crook anyhow. I don't imagine almost a whole town—and you—can be wrong about him. But there's got to be proof that'll stand up in a court of law. When that happens, you'll be more than welcome at the trial."

"Proof? Why?" Ione snapped the ends of her reins against her skirt-covered leg with a dull staccato sound that made her horse dance. "Nobody needed proof when they murdered Isaac. I stuck my neck out and found this operation for you, Mr. Osgood. But it sounds to me like you're not going to do anything except talk. Talk, talk, talk! You're going to sit on the fence and waffle, while that evil man gets away with murder, aren't you?"

He flinched, her scathing opinion of him burning like a brand in his gut. He clenched his hands over his saddle horn and spoke calmly, as though what she said didn't matter, didn't hurt. "If you won't go home, Ione, go back to town. I can't work and fret about you, too."

"Don't tell me what to do." Her voice, instead of rising, lowered almost to a whisper. "I'm going to find my son's killer, with or without your help. I know this operation is proof of O'Doud's thievery. I can feel it in my bones. It's the reason Blodgett and Isaac were murdered, and you're crazy if you think I'm going to ride home like a frightened rabbit while you're out talking and the evidence disappears."

Osgood's own temper was starting to rise. Heat mounted the back of his neck. "You let me worry about the evidence. But here's something for you to chew on, Mrs. Gilpatrick. Even if O'Doud has been stealing timber, it doesn't automatically prove he killed Blodgett or finagled your son's execution. I'm the peace officer here. I can't run off half-cocked like some flighty kid chasing every rumor. I have to work within the law."

"Flighty kid? Who do you mean, Isaac or me?" White-faced, Ione stared at him. He ached for her, for her outrage and her pain, but it was true. He'd been a lawman for most of his life, and a good one, even when the drink was in him. He'd been careless once. He never would be again.

"You miserable coward." Her words cut through him. Whirling her piebald pony, she dug her heel into its side and lashed out with the reins. The horse lunged forward and although Osgood called her name, she didn't answer. The thud of the pony's hooves died away, leaving him surrounded by silence, dark trees, and a cloudy patch of sky overhead.

It was like the world had emptied, and so had he.

***

SHAME SOON BROUGHT Ione to her senses. Shame for spurring her cayuse to a breakneck pace over the uneven ground, and yes, shame, too, for calling the marshal a coward. She knew him better than that already. The regret did not, however, erase her anger toward him one whit. Old as she was, she felt like sitting down and howling like a child. Better to brush the tears from her cheeks and whip up some righteous anger.

How dare Marshal TJ Osgood send her away like he had? He must be aware they were within a hair's breadth of uncovering answers to all the questions he said must be cleared. The evidence that would nail O'Doud's hide to the wall and avenge her son's murder was sitting right in front of him. She knew it was. And she wanted in on the final chapter. She deserved to be.

But what was he doing? Protecting her, TJ said, but if she hadn't had the good sense and inner determination to follow Jensen out here this morning, this unlawful operation might well have gone undiscovered for who knows how long. And now what did the marshal plan to do? Why, ask more questions, he said. Investigate all avenues for a foolproof case.

Yet it almost seemed to her as though he were trying to prove O'Doud innocent, not guilty. And if he did that, Isaac's murderer would go free.

Ione's thoughts spun around and round, like a bug captive in a jar. They jumped among resentment, anger, a tiny bit of understanding for Osgood's point of view, then back again. The only constant was her steadfast determination to bring justice to her son. So deeply was she concentrating on ways and mean, she paid scant attention to the thud of her mare's hooves on the soft forest floor, or the quiet twitter of birds and buzz of late season insects.

It was the sound of distant gunshots that roused her. They carried from the woods she'd left behind, although from what precise direction she was unable to tell.

Her stomach clenched in sudden fear for Osgood. Had he run into trouble? But as quickly as they'd begun, the shots died away and all was silent again. Presently, when nothing more happened, her start of fear faded, along with the fierce anger fueling her rage. Soothed by the susurrus music playing in the tree tops, she patted the mare's neck and started off again.

She was nearly home before she figured out she was being followed.

Chapter 12

MISERABLE COWARD. Osgood tried to tell himself she hadn't meant it, but he knew she had. Meant the contempt, if not the literal meaning. His own fault. He'd handled her badly in seeming to devalue her help.

He kept his horse under a tight rein, preventing the animal from following Ione's pony. Best, he figured, that she remain angry with him, and so avoid him for the next few days. Let her cool off slowly over time.

It was easy to find excuses for her attack. She was distraught, her nerves strained to breaking from the obscene method in which her son had died. Lashing out at him was the only way she had of purging her anger. Maybe, he told himself, he should be relieved it was he she'd gone after, and not O'Doud.

If she hadn't gone after O'Doud. It was beyond him to predict what she might do. Any woman bold enough to take employment with a man she suspected of being a murderer—with the intention of spying on him and the men in his employ—was a sight more daring than he cared to speculate on.

Miserable coward. Her epitaph resounded in his head again and again as he gigged his horse in the ribs and methodically began following the skid marks the lumberjacks had left. Was it true? Did his reluctance to condemn O'Doud out-of-hand stem from caution, or was it from some ingrained sense of fairness? He favored the sense of fairness. The law was the law, and he the law's advocate. If there was proof of the man's involvement, he'd find it and present the evidence to the county sheriff in Coeur d'Alene City. And Ione Gilpatrick, when she came to her senses, would be glad. Deep down, she was that kind of woman.

He only hoped she was headed home, out of danger. And that she would come to trust him.

Osgood came upon the log decks without warning, three of them stacked as much as twenty feet high. Inexperienced though he was in the logging business, he could tell the lumber would be graded select. Cut into sixteen-foot sections, and each with approximately a three-foot diameter, the logs were knot-free their entire length. Whoever cut them, had taken only the best part of the tree and left the rest to rot.

No human was around, or even a bit of gear, but there was a bull elk with an impressive set of antlers grazing between two of the decks. As Osgood neared, it whistled and darted into the deep woods. Must have mistaken him for a hunter, Osgood figured. A few seconds later, he was the one who jumped as, off to his left, three or four blue grouse flew up into a tree on a thunder of beating wings.

The Little North Fork must have been near because he smelled water, and if he pricked his ears, he fancied he heard the burble and gush of a fast running stream. It should've been soothing—but it wasn't. He had an itch between his shoulder blades that made him long to put his back against the rough bark of a tree and scratch like an old mule. And then stay there with the tree for protection.

Osgood couldn't help wondering if this was how Blodgett had felt in the moments before he died. Or had the old marshal been oblivious until the final moment?

Those blue grouse—they'd flown for a reason, and it wasn't because he'd bothered them. Without fanfare, he switched the reins into his left hand, leaving his right free to draw the.44. Immediately, he sensed a change. An atmosphere already crackling with tension grew more heavy and sullen, if that were possible. His old partner had been known to laugh at Osgood, calling him a wizard on account of the way he could sense danger reaching for him. He felt danger now, trying to gather him in.

Osgood set spur to his horse at the same instant the echoing report of a rifle shook the needles on the trees. A bullet cut chunks of bark from one of the logs as the gelding sprang into the lea of the deck. Without bothering to aim, Osgood returned fire, guessing at the direction from which the bullet had come, only to have a hail of lead spray around him fast as the shooter could jack in bullets. He slid to the ground beside the horse, making as small a target of himself as possible.

The woods remained devoid of movement, although he saw burned powder smoke spreading in a low cloud over a deadfall. He shot into the lowest, upwind end of the cloud, hoping to get lucky.

Silence fell again. Osgood emptied the spent shells from his pistol, refilled the chambers and waited, motionless and patient.

What if Ione had been with him? He shuddered at the idea. She hadn't liked him doing so, but in sending her away, he might well have saved her life. Oh, he was a coward all right. He'd learned the hard way that you can't put other folks at risk, even if the end result is for the greater good. Not if you ever wanted to sleep at night.

He hunkered, wrapping the reins around his wrist. Once, far off, he was aware of some small commotion, more guessed at than heard. His ambusher, leaving as silently as he'd come and chasing down that elk?

Or was that what he wanted Osgood to think?

Enduring as dirt, Osgood ticked off another five minutes by his cheap silver pocket watch. When nothing further happened, he poked a small tree limb with his hat stuck on top around the side of the log deck. The grouse, he saw, had fluttered from their perches and were digging in the ground like persnickety farmers, their fright over. Feeling like a fool, he settled his Stetson on his head and mounted the horse.

Whoever had shot at him hadn't stayed around long enough to be interesting. Osgood still felt uneasy, although the itchy place on his back had disappeared. He didn't reckon there was anything more here to find.

His next step was to talk to this Finley feller Ione had told him about. See if the logging operation had any basis in legality. If it did, he'd need to look elsewhere for his proof. If it didn't, he'd be stepping up due process.

***

OSGOOD ENTERED TOWN from the same direction he'd left it, dropping his horse off at the stables and hiking over to the office on foot. He found his deputy taking things easy. Benny's bare feet were propped on the wood box, his round face slack in sleep. The mongrel dog lay beside him. The only one to take notice when Osgood came in, Badger opened an eye and yawned.

It was a scene similar to his first night here, although Osgood had learned by now that his deputy's softness hid a solid core.

The holding cell wasn't empty. It held a single prisoner. Johansson was stretched out on the lower bunk—the blanket tented up over his wounded leg—and he was snoring in drugged sleep.

Deliberately, Osgood tilted the rocking chair forward, jarring his young deputy awake.

"What's he doing here?" Osgood cocked a thumb toward Johansson. "He's supposed to be at Doc's."

152

"Doc Worthy don't want him. He tried to wrassle Doc down and get away. I got over there just in time to kick his good leg out from under him. Changed his mind, I can tell you, long enough for Doc to pour another dose of laudanum into him. We figured if he felt as lively as all that, he needed to be in the lock-up."

Osgood approved his deputy's, and the doctor's, good sense. "I see the other fellers got hauled off. Everything go all right with them?"

"Yeah. Them Coeur d'Alene men said they needed a day off tomorrow, Marshal. They're planning on going to church." Tompko grinned. "What did you find out? Miz Gilpatrick point you in the right direction?"

"Inconclusive." Osgood poured himself a cup of coffee that'd been on the stove so long it was thick as pudding, and sank into the chair behind his desk. "Although, since I got shot at again, I'm inclined to believe she knows what she's talking about."

"Shot at? Weren't hit, were you?" Benny stumbled to his feet, looking around as though searching for an enemy. When none materialized, and at Osgood's reassurance that the shooter had missed, he sat down again. "Well, did you get a look at him?"

"Nary a peep. He was too far away and under good cover. Might as well've been a ghost." Disgusted all over again, Osgood rocked his chair back on two legs and closed his eyes for a moment. Every blow he'd taken in the fight, every sleepless hour of the previous night's watch, and every mile of the ride today was making itself felt. And he never had gotten that hot bath.

Sighing, he forced himself out of the chair, catching at the corner of the desk as his bad leg buckled. Life was getting to be one annoyance piled on another.

"Where do I find this Finley who owns the land southeast of O'Doud's? Ione...Mrs. Gilpatrick said he lives in town."

If Tompko caught Osgood's use of Ione's given name, he found nothing amiss in it. Maybe he was too sleepy, for he yawned, scratched an armpit and gave the marshal succinct directions to Black Crossing's best rooming house.

On the way there, Osgood stopped off at the post office and checked out the map of claimed land. Sure enough, although some of the original settlers' holdings had been traded or sold, their names scratched out and replaced, Finley was still listed as the owner of the land where the logs had been cut.

He found Finley at home. A middle-aged man, he'd gone to fat, due in part, as he told Osgood when they shook hands, "Because I can't do any real work anymore." His leg was off just below the hip, the stump too short for him to wear his wooden leg for more than brief periods. A pair of crutches stood propped by his chair. Seeing him up close, Osgood knew him for one of the wags who weekdays hung out with Meredith over at the Chain and Choker.

"What's that you say?" Besides being fat and with only one leg, he was hard of hearing. His barely subdued shout carried a strong English accent. "Do I still own my land? I most certainly do. I came to this country for land, and what I've got, I'll keep."

"That's fine, Mr. Finley," Osgood said. "But what about the trees on the land? Have you sold any timber lately, or maybe the logging rights?"

Finley's eyes narrowed in shrewd regard. "Of course not. The land is only worth what's growing on it. Once the timber is gone, this mountain ground won't grow anything but huckleberries. It's too high for crops and there aren't any minerals worth mining. Might run a few head of cattle if the ticks don't eat 'em alive. That's why I'm saving what I've got for my old age." He stopped and tapped his brown-colored front teeth with a horny fingernail. "What makes you ask, Mr. Osgood?"

Osgood purely did hate telling a crippled man his future welfare was compromised. Finley took it better than expected, sitting in stunned silence before cutting loose with a few well-chosen and imaginative curses.

"So you're telling me I'm ruined, that about the size of it?" His hands, still bearing heavy calluses from using an axe and saw, clenched. "You're saying once I'm out of cash I'll be headed for that poor farm over by Spangle?"

"I'm no expert," Osgood said, "but I don't think it's that drastic yet. Now I know what's going on, you can count on me putting a stop to it."

"What I'm hoping is that you can nail the thieves and I can get my money back."

"Do my best." Osgood figured that was unlikely. He stood, but Finley halted him with a gesture.

"Would it do any good to ask who the thief is?"

Osgood avoided his eyes. "I've got a suspect, Mr. Finley. But I'll need proof before I can move on him."

"I think we both know who the chief suspect is, and he's always been able to buy his way out anything." Finley shook his head. "So I'd say this is a case of the law complicating justice. This have anything to do with that fight last night? Or Blodgett's murder, or the kid those crooks out of Wallace hanged?"

"Maybe," Osgood said. "I'm waiting to see if the ends tie into a square knot is all."

"I hope they do." Finley reached for his crutches and heaved his bulk out of the chair to see Osgood to the door. "I truly hope they do."

Osgood didn't think there was anybody hoped it more than he did. Excepting, of course, Ione Gilpatrick.

On his way back to the marshal's office, the smells wafting from the café enticed him inside before he could get past the door. An aroma of roasting meat, baking bread and chocolate all mixed together served to remind Osgood he hadn't eaten since his interrupted breakfast. Without thinking twice, he sat down at what was rapidly becoming his usual supper table.

Magda came over to take his order, smoothing her flowered apron around her neat waist. "What vill you have, Marshal?" Her smile was as perfunctory as her question.

Osgood perused the chalkboard menu, which confirmed what his nose had told him. "A chunk of elk roast and a big piece of the chocolate cake, please, Magda. I'm almost hungry enough to eat the hide that elk was wearing."

The quip didn't raise a twinkle, let alone a smile.

"Comin' right up." She hurried into the kitchen to confer with Mrs. Tenney.

Osgood, puzzled by her cool reception, couldn't guess why she'd walked off so fast. He'd been looking forward to a bit of conversation that had no uncomfortable undertones to it. Only one other table was occupied at this early hour, yet for the first time since he'd arrived in Black Crossing, she appeared to have no time to talk.

Which was all right with him. He rubbed his eyes, too weary to think much about the snub, finding it difficult to stay awake long enough for his grub to arrive. And, as much as he dreaded the idea, he'd need to remain alert until the wee hours of the morning. It was Saturday night. Time for the backcountry lumberjacks to cut loose and celebrate their survival of another week in the woods.

While staring after Magda in bewilderment, his gaze came to rest on the two men at the other table. One, whom Osgood had never seen before, was a lugubrious looking individual with an upturned mustache and a down-turned mouth. His neck and shoulders were as thick as a bull's; even sitting he appeared a half-foot taller than Osgood.

The other man was Jensen.

Whatever they were talking about must have been important—and secret—if he were to gather anything from the way they cupped their hands around their mouths, hiding the movement of their lips. It piqued Osgood's interest. Whatever they were discussing, he judged he must have played a part since it seemed his interest was reciprocated. At least by Jensen, whose beady eyes watched Osgood's every movement. All he could see of the stranger was the side of his face.

Magda came over and placed a small bowl of soup in front of him.

"Who is that with Jensen?" Osgood inquired, quietly thanking her.

"Shh," she whispered. "Don't ask me no questions." She was gone before he could pick up his spoon, let alone ask what she meant. While he made short work of the soup, he saw her stop at the other table and pick up their used bowls. The men were noticeable in their silence until she left again.

The mystery of Magda's new attitude was solved when Jensen and his dinner companion paid their bill and left. Magda's smile glistened as she refilled Osgood's coffee mug.

"That Jensen," she said, "he wass asking about you. He wass thinkin' my Benny talks about you, but I told him he don't. My Benny sleeps most nights at the jail, I told him. I said I didn't know nuthin'."

"What did he want to know about me?" Osgood's sense of threat snapped to attention.

"He wants to know if you carry a hideout gun. He wants to know if you carry a knife. He wants to know if you're a fast drawer. A drawer—ist that right?" Without letting him answer, she hurried on. "As if I would know! But what iss a fast drawer?"

"Reckon he wanted to know if I'm any good as a gunman. What did you tell him?"

Magda's blue eyes twinkled and she laughed. "I tell him when you sit down to eat, I hear metal clankin'. I tell him I think you are dangerous." She sobered. "I do not like Mr. Jensen, or that other man who does not look me in the eye." There was a pause before she added, "Then Jensen, he asked about Mrs. Gilpatrick."

Osgood's blood chilled. "Ione? What for? What did he ask you?"

Magda's mouth puckered and she shook her head. "He asks if she hass got any money. He asks if she stays at her house alone. He asks where is her house. He asks how old she iss, and what does she look like. I say to him, 'I do not know.' I say, 'You should talk to her yourself.'"

If Osgood thought his blood had chilled before, he could feel ice running through his veins now. "I wish you hadn't told him that, Magda. Did he want to know anything else?"

"No. He says he guess he will go talk to her himself."

Osgood scooted his chair back with a scraping of its legs. "That's bad, Magda. That's real bad. I'm going to have to ride out to her place and persuade her to come into town where she'll be safe."

Magda nearly dropped the fifty-cent coin he handed her, her expression startled. "Safe? Iss she in danger?"

She might as well saved her breath since the only audience was Osgood's back. Leaving his coffee untouched, he hastened towards the door.

Benny jumped to his feet at Osgood's precipitate entrance. The marshal was explaining the situation and issuing orders before Tompko had a chance to say a word.

"Go get her," Osgood said. He'd reluctantly put aside his idea of riding to Ione's rescue himself. Her anger would still be hot and, given her earlier attitude, she'd be unlikely to listen to anything he said. "Bring her in, whether she wants to come or not."

"You bet I'll go," Benny agreed readily, pulling on his shoes. "I know where she lives. You're apt to get turned around after sunset."

Osgood couldn't argue. Night comes early in big timber country, especially in the autumn. He might easily lose his way and there was no time for him to be stumbling around in the dark. Better, although he chafed at the necessity, if Benny persuaded Ione to come stay in town where Osgood could protect her. At least she wasn't mad at Benny.

"Get a move on," Osgood said. "Tell Leonard over at the livery I said to give you a good horse. A fast horse." The memory of the commotion he'd heard out on the trail after he'd been shot at, the one he'd passed off as the spooked elk, came back to haunt him. He'd believed the shooter had been after him, but had he also seen Ione as she was leaving?

Benny had his coat on. At the last moment, he turned to the marshal. "Should I take a rifle?"

Grim-faced, Osgood pulled the gun down off the wall-rack and added a box of cartridges. "Be careful, Benny. And hurry."

"It's not far to the Gilpatrick place," Benny tried to reassure him. "I'll have her back here in an hour or so."

"Make it less," Osgood said. He'd never been good at waiting, something that had been known to trip him up when he was in the detecting business. It was no easier on him now.

Not being one to sit around and chew his fingernails to no purpose, Osgood soon gave up on pacing the office floor to splinters and took to the streets instead. It was Saturday night. There were still his regular rounds to be made. The local saloons had their usual problems that needed solving. Drunks to get off the street and out of the alleys, arguments in need of mediation, as well as more than a few brawls to break up—although he was careful to avoid getting in the middle of any of those. The fracas last night would do him for a spell.

Although most everyone had heard of his clash with O'Doud's logging crew—and consequently grown leery of taking on Marshal TJ Osgood—it wasn't long before his lone cell filled with men sitting on the floor, all crowded together leaving the bunk to Johansson.

One was a man he'd caught urinating in the middle of the street and weeping as though his heart would break. Another, whom he'd cautioned twice about swearing in a voice loud as a bullhorn, had proceeded to ignore the marshal's warnings. The last man, one whose idea of a fair fight involved pitting an

Arkansas toothpick against bare fist, completed the roster. He'd objected to his plaything being taken away and Osgood had been forced to pistol whip some sense into him.

By now, Osgood hardly noticed he was tired, what with drinking cup after cup of coffee strong enough to float an anvil, and his nerves growing more and more frayed while he waited for Deputy Tompko's return.

He did notice, however, that Badger had detected his jitters and was following him as he paced the street. Osgood appreciated the dog's company, especially as first the hour Tompko had mentioned crawled past and then another.

***

AS IONE REACHED the cutoff heading for home, an intense sensation of being watched penetrated her anger. It didn't seem wise to disregard the feeling, so giving in to it, she let her subconscious take over. Fighting the inclination that told her to run for the cabin, she pulled her mare to a halt, patting the horse's neck as though giving it a rest. Then artfully, like a tourist admiring the scenery and the late afternoon weather, sunny after the days of rain, she glanced around.

Her back trail was clear, as far as she could see. The woods ahead were alive with birds, bugs and small animals, but the wood behind? Silent. Too silent perhaps? She saw no one, perceived no movement, although the feeling stayed with her.

"What about it, Nellie?" she murmured to her companion. "Am I imagining things?"

The cayuse whuffled and shook her head, rattling the bit in her mouth.

"No," Ione said. "I don't think so either." She should have listened to TJ, she acknowledged, now when it was too late. She should have trusted him and not let her pique make her careless. Ignoring the urge to flee, she remained level-headed enough not to be stampeded into leading any bushwhackers to her cabin. Why else had she been so careful to keep her identity secret? Let no one know where she lived?

At her urging, Nellie ambled forward again as though they had all the time in the world. There was another logging road splitting off from this one a couple hundred yards beyond their turnoff, she recalled. And if she followed that, she would soon come to yet another branch, and then another. A circuitous route, to be sure, but one guaranteed to lead whoever was following her a merry chase. If she kept to the grassy verge and made no sign of passage, the watcher would soon be left behind, her trail lost.

The next curve in the road provided the opportunity she was looking for. Nellie broke into a run as Ione gigged her. They reached the split in the road, Ione guiding the mare into the brushy entrance. The stalker would soon find where she'd ducked off, but he'd be slowed down.

For the first time she wondered if the person following her was Osgood, then discarded the thought. No. Even if he were being secretive, she would not be this afraid. Although it didn't make any sense, she knew that was so.

"Come on, Nellie," she whispered. "Let's fly."

Nellie did her best.

Chapter 13

RESTLESS AND UNABLE TO UNWIND, Osgood checked his prisoners, paying strict attention to the crier he'd caught urinating in the street—much to the dismay of Magda's café patrons who had a first-class view. He found all the men sleeping, if not quiet. Draining the coffee pot dregs into his cup, he began stewing over Tompko and Ione's overdue arrival in earnest. Benny must be having a difficult time in persuading her to come in. That was the best face he could put on the delay.

Ione wouldn't refuse to take shelter in town, would she? An intelligent woman, she must have gotten over being angry with him by now. She was bound to see reason. Damn it all! He couldn't protect her if she stayed out of town while his duties kept him in Black Crossing.

Two hours and more passed before Benny arrived, his horse lathered from running. He was alone.

Osgood, forgetting his sore leg, hurried out to meet him, hoping against hope the reason Tompko was by himself was because Ione had found someone trustworthy to take her in. But, as he laid a firm hand on Benny's reins and stared up at his white-faced young deputy, he knew that wasn't so.

"Well?" he demanded, a sinking feeling in the pit of his stomach.

"She ain't there, sir." Benny swallowed. "And her cabin is all tore up."

The muscles in Osgood's chest tightened as though somebody had thrown a lasso around him and yanked the rope taut. "Not there? She's gone?"

"G…gone." Tompko could barely speak.

"Her horse, too?" Osgood felt his heart accelerate like a locomotive leaving the station, although he forced an impassive façade to show his wild-eyed deputy, hoping to calm the young man. "A scrawny piebald mare."

"I don't know."

"Think, Benny. Did you look for her out at the barn? Or at the corrals or the outbuildings?"

"I looked everywhere, Marshal," Tompko said. "And she ain't got a barn, just a shed with room for her horse." The deputy's eyes rolled up in their sockets, as if that would help him remember. At last, he said, "No. The mare wasn't there. But, Marshal, her things was all thrown around. Her food supplies, cooking utensils. Every last thing. The bed mattress was cut up, and even her unmentionables was tossed out in plain sight."

The idea of her unmentionables seemed to shock him more than anything.

Osgood figured he had a better grasp of why her cabin had been violated than Tompko, and he liked the concept even less than his deputy.

"Any blood?" he asked, after a pause. The horse he was holding sensed the man's tension and trembled.

Benny's fair skin whitened a shade more above the beginnings of his blond beard. "No, sir. I'd have noticed that right off."

"How about tracks? Any sign which way whoever tore her place up went?"

Tompko looked desperate at the question. "Marshal! I don't know. It's dark. I couldn't see."

Osgood opened his mouth to speak, rethought the inclination, and closed it again. He'd better not go blaming Tompko for what had happened—for what might have happened—to Ione Gilpatrick. It was his fault, sure as God made alligators green. His fault, once again, just like his old detective partner's death. Only this time he didn't have whiskey as an excuse for his carelessness. This time he'd plain been stupid. He'd known she shouldn't ride off alone from back there in the woods where she shouldn't ought to have been, and when he took a stubborn stand about fairness and justice and letting the law take its course, he'd failed her. He'd let her ride straight into danger.

"What took you so long getting back here?" he asked Tompko, the anger in him burning white hot. "Shouldn't have taken more than two hours to report."

"I rode around in the woods for a bit," Tompko said. "Calling for her, in case she was hiding out someplace near. But she never answered, so I reckon she wasn't."

Osgood didn't think so either. She was either dead or taken, neither of which boded well for her, but at least Tompko hadn't found a body. He felt hollow inside, thinking of the head start her assailants had, although he remained expressionless for his deputy's sake. "If she couldn't see you, she might not answer, Benny. Or maybe she did know it was you, but was afraid if she yelled, whoever messed with her house could get to her before you."

"I'm gonna head over to her cabin again first thing in the morning," Tompko promised. "I'll ride out before sunup."

"We both will." He wouldn't take any more prisoners tonight, Osgood decided. They could rob any store, or burn the damn place down, and he wouldn't care. He'd loose the prisoners he had in a few hours, without laying a charge. Ione Gilpatrick was a much bigger concern than a few lumberjacks, each on bent on proving himself the biggest bull of the woods.

He slapped Benny's livery mount on the rump, urging it toward the barn. "Go get some sleep, Tompko. We'll find her tomorrow."

***

NELLIE HAD BEEN SWEATING a little when they reached the clearing where Ione's cabin stood, though no more than Ione. Pausing in the shelter of the woods, Ione waited a few minutes, watching to making certain her cabin was as untouched as it seemed.

Must be safe, she finally decided, observing the half-dozen chickens scratching in the dirt around the coop. If she stayed in this country, she would get some geese—or a dog. Better a dog like Isaac had meant to do, for the company as well as warning of strangers. A hunter, trained to protect him. Too late.

She rode on in, her triumph over eluding her pursuer fading into sadness.

"But we're getting good at this, aren't we, Nellie?" She pulled the saddle from the mare, setting it on its side in the shed, and found a brush. "Soon we'll be like wild Indians, running here and there without need of roads or civilization. We'll go where we want, free as the breeze. Just as soon as Colin O'Doud is out of business."

Brave words she was no longer sure she believed, though the mare whickered agreeably as Ione brushed the sweat and dirt from her back. What she did believe was that her time here was running out. She may have gotten away this time, but soon O'Doud's men would find her lair and realize she was Isaac's mother. Then, depending on what she'd discovered—or what he thought she'd discovered—O'Doud would either have her killed, just like Isaac, or see she was run out of town, her reputation in shreds.

But not, she thought fiercely, if she had anything to say about it.

Once inside the cabin, she thrust a stick of wood into the stove and set about preparing a meager supper of warmed-over stew and cold biscuits. It was enough. She wasn't hungry anyway. A wry smile crooked her mouth. Just as well since she was about out of supplies.

Loneliness set in, and she wondered if she had the nerve to go into town after dark and speak to Osgood. Apologize maybe because the fright of being followed had let her see he had his point regarding her involvement. To him, she was just someone else he had to worry about. Misguided worry, but perhaps it wasn't fair of her. Besides, if he'd had time to talk to Finley, perhaps he had a clearer direction in which to go, and she really could safely leave retribution to him.

With a tired sigh, she drew a homemade chair up to the table and picked up her fork, then was shocked by the sudden blast of the cabin door as it crashed open on its hinges. Two men stood there, leering in at her and cutting off any escape—one of the men was Jensen; the other a very large stranger. She might have known.

"Well, well," Jensen said, sauntering over to the table where she sat as if glued, fork still poised over her food. "If it isn't Mrs. Fane, living in Isaac Gilpatrick's cabin as big as life. Who'd ever of thought? I suppose you're his ma."

Her chin lifted. "Yes." She stood up, grateful that her wobbly knees supported her.

He reached into the cast iron Dutch oven and dipped out a ladle of stew, eating from the utensil and smacking his lips. "Tasty," he pronounced, but deposited a second ladleful on the table. That must not have been enough mess because deliberately, watching her reaction, he dumped the rest of the pot there as well. That didn't satisfy him either. He overturned the table, sending her crockery plate to the floor where it shattered into a hundred pieces, splattering her skirt with stew.

"A waste of good food," she said. Her voice came out dry and cracked. One foot length at a time, she edged backward toward the stove as though seeking warmth. Isaac's rifle was there, if only she could reach it.

"The boss ain't going to like this," Jensen said, advancing on her. A vague gesture encompassed the cabin, her, the world. "He's don't like being fooled the way you done. Coming right into his own home and spying on him—on us. I suppose you're the one told the marshal where to find the log decks over at Finley's. Well, you got away with it for a while, but it was easy enough to trail you home. Just took a while, what with everything else."

Did he mean TJ was dead? Ione heart clenched and she kept retreating. For every step she took, he followed.

"Guess it came natural for the kid to be a goody two-shoes," he said.

Ione lifted her head. "If you are referring to Isaac's honesty and decency, I guess it did."

Jensen's hand lashed out, catching her on the cheekbone. She stumbled, nearly fell as pain traveled all the way down to her toes.

"Miss Selah's been bawling like a sick calf all day," Jensen continued his tirade. "Driving us crazy. She's saying you stole something from her. She won't say what, mind you, but I'm gonna take it back. Shut her up."

"She's mistaken," Ione said coldly. "I took nothing of hers."

Jensen chuckled, his thin lips never curving. "Lady, Miss Selah is never mistaken." He looked over at the other man. "Covich, you got any ideas on what to do with a spy? Aside from shooting her at dawn."

Covich shrugged. "Take her to San Francisco. Soon Yee'll pay top dollar for a good-looking woman like her. Drug her until she can't see straight and slap her around 'til she knows he means business, then put her to work in his Red Dragon House."

He blocked the door. Ione had no where to run and in truth, her legs would hardly support her as it was.

"Got any of those drugs on you?" Jensen asked.

Covich smiled. "Of course. Got a twist of good quality opium right in my pocket. Get a dose of that in her and she'll come along meek as a lamb."

Ione's back was against the wall, braced there, as she prepared herself to fight. They thought to make her a whore? Stuff her with drugs until she was helpless? Not while there was a spark of resistance left in her!

But, in the end, there wasn't much she could do against two men such as Covich and Jensen. Except stab Jensen in the muscle between his neck and his shoulder with the fork still in her hand. There was that much satisfaction. The surprisingly high-pitched scream he emitted before they overwhelmed her was music to her ears.

It didn't make things right, though. She'd been aiming for his eyes.

***

LONG BEFORE DAWN, Osgood thrust himself out of bed. He washed and shaved by lamplight, and put on his last clean shirt. Almost, he told himself wryly, as if he were on a mission to rescue a princess like in one of those myths or fairy tales. The alternative he wouldn't admit, even to himself. The one that said he might not find Ione in time. Could be he'd best be prepared to meet his Maker. But he'd abide by that, if it was what fate decreed, as long as he got Ione Gilpatrick out alive. As long as she wasn't already dead.

The men they were up against played rough, as a glimpse of his own face in the tiny mirror proved. One eye was bloodshot from a broken vein, his bruises gone from red, to purple, to vivid green and yellow. The ones on his body were even worse he saw now he had his shirt off. And there was a knob on his forehead that made him think it was a good thing he had a thick skull—although he supposed there were folks who'd argue the point.

Benny stumbled into the office soon after Osgood got there. "I'm taking the rifle," he announced, fetching it down from the rack where it was kept.

"Go ahead." Osgood had his holstered Smith & Wesson, his.25 pocket pistol at his back, and a double-barreled shotgun to carry in his saddle scabbard. "I want you to get on down to the livery and saddle the horses, Benny." He picked up the cell door key and limped toward the hallway. His bad leg was giving him fits today, hard to ignore. "I'll roust the prisoners out. Don't want any loose ends here in town."

"No, sir." Benny's face, drawn and looking much older than his seventeen or eighteen years, brightened with a grin. "They're going to be mighty surprised. They always had to pay a fine before we'd turn them loose."

We. Osgood supposed he meant old Marshal Blodgett and himself. "Not this time."

He was a bit surprised at the complaints he got as he wakened the prisoners and told them they were free to go. Complaints—plus he got batted in his sore face by one of the men who wasn't done sleeping off the effects of his Saturday night bender.

"Whaddya mean, out?" queried the feller he'd run in on account of his language where women and children were present. "Where's our breakfast? We always get breakfast. Comes as part of the deal."

"Tell you what," Osgood said, helping the unsteadiest of the three to stay on his feet. "I'll forego the fine, and you can buy your own breakfast. If Magda will let you in her café."

He opened his untidy desk drawer, rifled through the contents until he found the men's possessions and handed over guns, knives and any money they'd been carrying with no regard for who owned what. Let them sort stuff out. There wasn't much to argue over.

"All right, boys," he said. "Vamoose on out of here. Next time, I won't be so lenient." If, he reminded himself, he lived long enough for there to be a next time.

Johansson, from the bunk, complained at the noise, but fell back to sleep as soon as the others were gone. Meredith and Doc Worthy could be depended on to look in on him later.

***

THE SUN WAS RISING above the treetops as Tompko led them into Ione Gilpatrick's yard. Located a couple of miles out of Black Crossing, they had reached her cabin by heading directly over the mountain behind Osgood's cabin, then taking a brushy, overgrown logging track north. Osgood never would have found the place without his deputy.

Ione's home was a three-room cabin that might have been built by the same man who'd thrown up Osgood's in town. But inside, there was a larger main room that took up more space than his entire cabin, with two cubbyholes partitioned off. Each of the tiny rooms held a bed, a stool and in Ione's case, a small bureau.

"It ain't much of a place," Benny said, as if he were apologizing for it. "Not fit for a lady like Miz Gilpatrick. It's just an old logger's cabin her and Isaac fixed up a little after she got here."

As Tompko had reported last night, the place had been systematically wrecked, with food strewn over the floor, stuffing escaping from the slashed bed-ticking, and Ione's bureau drawers emptied and tossed about. More chilling was the .270 rifle laying behind the door, the barrel bent into the letter C. How had that happened? he wondered, put off by the sight. It seemed nothing was sacrosanct, the devastation complete. Even the mice had been emboldened enough to add their mark to the chaos.

Whoever had done this had carried Ione away with him—or them. Osgood wondered what had gone through her mind when she saw what had been done. Did they force her to watch the destruction? Or, came a thought he did his best to quash, had they killed her and carried only a body away?

Osgood found no blood, which he thought was an encouraging sign. He also found nothing in the house to say who might have done the ransacking. Outside, it was something of a different story. Once he separated the tracks of both Ione's pony and the horse Tompko had ridden last night from the mix surrounding the house, a clearer picture formed in front of him. There were two men. One rode a tall, long-legged animal that was a little clumsy. Perhaps it hadn't been properly shod, for he found several places where the horse had apparently stumbled over air. The second horse took shorter strides, and the off front shoe was missing two nails. Tompko gaped at Osgood, watching him work out the story the tracks revealed.

"Say," he said, "think you can teach me how to track?"

"Maybe." Osgood concentrated. "This way," he said at last, turning his horse south and east, toward the river. Birds twittered in the underbrush, and small nocturnal hunters were returning to their nests or lairs after the early morning hunt when he and Tompko headed out. The day promised a little warmth as the sun peeked through broken clouds. A heavy dew kept scents close to the ground.

"Should've brought the dog," he said. "Maybe he could've trailed their horses. Been a lot faster."

"Could be." Tompko looked doubtful. "I don't know. Badger ain't all hound, you know."

"He's not a deputy either, but he did a good job the other night." Osgood had to explain this remark, which won a grin from Benny. It kept them occupied as he deciphered the story the tracks had to tell.

He showed Benny the characteristics that identified the tracks to him, whereupon his deputy, being a bright young feller, was mostly able to pick out the trail on his own.

"Who are these people?" Benny asked. "Who's riding the parade horse, do you suppose?"

"I don't know the men," Osgood told him, "but I'll know the horses when I find them."

"Me, too, now," Benny said, his face bleak and determined.

It was good, Osgood thought. If anything happened to him, Tompko could go on alone. Although the first few miles were traversed at speed, there came a time when he held up his hand, caution slowing their headlong chase. Anther horse had joined the first three. It had a queer, prancing gait, the hoof prints stuttering in the soft, pine-needle strewn soil.

He said nothing to his deputy, but he had a feeling they were being watched from the moment they turned onto one of the old trails that crisscrossed these woods. That place between his shoulder blades began itching again, same as when he'd been scouting out the log decks. The feeling never let up as they moved along the trail, but dogged him with wolf-like intent. Osgood was sweating. Benny, he was glad to see, remained oblivious to the eerie sensation.

It was rising nine o'clock when a turn in the road forced recognition and Osgood realized where they were.

"Well, well," he murmured, reining in and allowing Tompko to draw up beside him. "Will you look at this?"

"What is it, Marshal?" Tompko gaped around, and judging by his vacant look, was at a loss as to what had caused the marshal's interest.

"Do you see where we are?"

Tompko's shoulders lifted and he shook his head.

Osgood smiled grimly. "This is the back road into O'Doud's place."

"Where somebody took that shot at you the other night?"

"The same. I was on the other road." He pointed out the exact spot. "And the shooter was just about where you are."

Benny stared around. "Good place for an ambush."

Osgood was surprised when the sense of being watched faded like somebody had blown out a match. He nudged his horse forward. "C'mon, Benny. Let's just see where this trail ends."

They moved boldly into the middle of the track. No need to be secretive, Osgood figured. He had no doubt they'd be expected wherever they finished up.

A few minutes later, they followed the hoof prints of Ione's pony, plus the other three, into O'Doud's yard, arriving in the back part of the meadow behind the barn. A multitude of tracks melded together here, the ones they trailed lost among them.

A manure pile, steam rising from its inner heat, appeared almost mountainous beside the barn's wide-open back door. Osgood picked up the tracks there, leading straight inside. O'Doud's old hostler, Art, stood in the opening watching their arrival, and blocking them from entering. He was leaning on a pitchfork.

"Must be the official welcoming committee," Osgood murmured to Benny.

"Yeah. Or the 'throw the bums out' committee," Benny replied.

Osgood walked his horse right up to the man, loosening the thong over his Smith & Wesson as he came. "Howdy, Art," he said. "I hope you're going to tell me who those men are that brought the woman here, and where she is now."

The old hostler's feet scuffed the dust. "Men?" he said, his eyes as shifty as his feet. "What men? What woman?"

Osgood pulled the pistol and leveled it at him. "Don't try to be cute, old-timer. It doesn't suit you. A blind man could follow the tracks they left."

"So what? I don't have to tell you anything, mister. What goes on here ain't any of your business."

Behind him, Osgood sensed, more than heard Tompko working at getting the rifle out of his scabbard.

"A woman being kidnapped makes it my business," he said. "If you don't want to spend the rest of your days in the hoosegow, I'd suggest you start talking."

"And make it fast," Tompko said, although nobody was listening to him. "We ain't got all day."

"Kidnapped?" The hostler's laugh sounded more like a nervous cough. "Nobody's been kidnapped. You got the wrong idea. There ain't no kidnapped woman. One set of those tracks belongs to Mrs. Fane. Mr. Jensen's had his eye on her for a long time, and now they're goin' off to get married. Mr. O'Doud tole me they was eloping, that's why they came in the back way. I even seen the boss give Jensen money before they left. That's all. You got no call to brandish that pistol at me."

Married. For just a flash, Osgood considered the possibility, and as quickly discarded it. He'd seen the job Jenson had done on Ione's cabin. He knew the gunslinger frightened, not thrilled her.

"Is that right?" he said. "Puzzles me on how you know so much about it. Quit wasting my time. Where are they?"

"They's gone. I don't know which way they went or where they was goin'."

Without turning his head away from the old duffer, Osgood motioned Tompko forward. "Check the stalls, Deputy. See if any of those horses are still here."

Although he had a pretty decent view of the stabled critters, he didn't trust Art not to make a try at thrusting the pitchfork through him the moment his back was turned. Benny nodded and shoved past him. In seconds, he was back.

"That fancy stepper is here," he said, excitement squeaking in his voice. "It's a palomino stallion with a bowed neck. The parade horse. Looks like the others rode out the front door."

"That palomino is Mr. O'Doud's Saddlebred," the hostler said indignantly. "It cost a lot of money. Of course it's here. You're bound to find its tracks. But Jensen and Mrs. Fane and that other feller has been gone for a couple hours."

Osgood stirred impatiently. Two hours? A sense of urgency was curling his guts into knots. Two hours gave Jensen an almost insurmountable lead. Anything could have happened to Ione by now—and his guess was none of it good.

"Who's the 'other' one?" he asked. He shoved his pistol into the holster, certain the old man wouldn't clam up now. Too full of himself, by far. Too happy to thwart the marshal.

"Dunno," the hostler replied. "Never seen him before. I thought maybe he was the preacher. He sure ain't no lumberjack."

Osgood stared hard at the hostler, until the man began to fidget. "He a tall, bull-like feller with a mustache?" he asked.

"Sounds like 'im."

"All right," the marshal said finally. He jerked his thumb. "Get back to work. Deputy, let's have a palaver with this man's boss."

"How'd you guess what that guy with Jensen looked like?" Tompko asked as they strode from the barn, leading their horses, while the hostler continued to lean on his pitchfork, watching. Osgood headed straight towards the house.

The marshal shrugged. "He was in your ma's place last night eating supper." He smiled briefly. "No mystery."

"Well then, who's this Mrs. Fane?" Tompko asked, his voice as bewildered as his face. He was right on Osgood's heels, dragging at his horse's reins.

"That's Mrs. Gilpatrick," Osgood said. "She took a different name when she got a job working for O'Doud so she could spy on him."

"Miz Gilpatrick went to work for O'Doud? How come you never told me before?"

"Figured the fewer people who knew, the less chance O'Doud would glom onto it."

Benny shook his head. "Holy smoke. Got a lot of ginger, ain't she?"

"Crazy woman, more like."

Osgood wrapped his bridle reins around the rail in front of the house, Benny following suit. Motioning the deputy to quiet, Osgood entered the house without so much as a by-your-leave. Certain of where he'd find O'Doud, he led his deputy down the hall to the office, their footsteps muffled by the carpet runner. The house was silent, the rooms cold.

Stopping in front of O'Doud's door, he pushed it open with the flat of his hand. O'Doud was seated at the desk. He glanced up without surprise, his hands occupied in rolling a pencil back and forth.

"Come in, Mr. Osgood," he said. Unnecessary, since Osgood was already in. "I've been expecting you."

Osgood knew he had, knew O'Doud had been watching from the woods.

"Then you also know what I'm doing here."

O'Doud rocked back in his chair. "Ah, yes. I rather think I do. You're looking for Mrs. Fane—better known to you as Mrs. Gilpatrick. The poor, deluded woman who believes her son was wrongfully hanged and that I somehow caused it. Tsk, tsk. Which is why my foreman is this minute escorting her, accompanied by the certifying doctor, of course, to an insane asylum in California where she'll be well cared for."

Osgood's belly clenched. He'd heard about those places. About how it was well nigh impossible to get a person out once he—or she—had been committed.

"You have no right—" he began.

"I have every right. Here's a woman who came into my home under false pretenses, using a fictitious name. She blames me for her son's troubles, and admits to wanting vengeance. She threatened me, Osgood, and she threatened my family. She even stole a rather valuable necklace from my daughter. Selah was terrified when she saw her here."

"Marshal!" Benny yelped a pained protest, as though Osgood could prevent what had already been said.

"Hush, Tompko." The funny part of O'Doud's speech, Osgood conceded, was that he was probably telling nothing more than the truth—or part of it. A truth turned upside down.

"We both know what's going on, O'Doud. Just like we both know you'll be going to prison for committing the identical crime Isaac Gilpatrick was hanged for. Mr. Finley will be pressing charges against the man who's been stealing his timber. I have proof you're the man. The charge isn't going to set well with any legitimate jury around here. You being mayor of Black Crossing is only going to make it worse in folk's eyes. It might go easier on you if you tell me where Jensen is taking Mrs. Gilpatrick."

O'Doud laughed. "Go easier on me? Osgood, you don't know what you're talking about."

"Salvage something from this mess," Osgood said, as though O'Doud hadn't spoken.

"Daddy!" Selah spoke from behind them. Benny whirled to face her, although she looked past him as if he were no more than a shadow on the wall. "What's going on? What is the marshal doing here? What about Ione?"

Osgood spoke before O'Doud could open his mouth. "I'm looking for her, Miss O'Doud. Have you seen her?"

"Why, yes." Selah's brow puckered. "A little while ago. She was with Mr. Jensen and another man."

She wore, Osgood noted, the same pink dress he seen previously.

"Be quiet, Selah," O'Doud said, tight and loud. He flapped his hands at her. "Go to your room. This doesn't concern you."

Seeing a mulish expression settle on the girl's sulky face, Osgood cut in quickly. "This is important, Selah. Ione is in danger. Where'd those men take her? Did you hear them say?"

"Selah!" O'Doud thundered, but his daughter was deaf to his anger.

"I don't know exactly." After one sly glance, Selah ignored her father. Her gaze fixed on Osgood, as though he was the only person with her in the room. "I saw Daddy gave Mr. Jensen quite a lot of money to pay their way on the train. They were going to catch it in Coeur d'Alene City. Jensen, Mrs. Fane and that other man—I heard Mr. Jensen call him Covich. I was frightened of him," she added. "I didn't like him being in the house."

O'Doud gave up trying to silence her. Osgood watched as the mayor sagged into his chair in defeat, hands resting on his thighs.

"The train to where?" Osgood asked.

She answered readily enough, glancing quickly, triumphantly at her father. "California, I think. San Francisco. I was very surprised. I'm sure Mrs. Fane doesn't like Mr. Jensen."

"And you'd be correct. My thanks, Miss O'Doud. I appreciate you telling me. Now maybe you'd best run along like your father said. I need to talk to him."

Selah smiled and pushed past Benny into the hall, the model of a well-behaved daughter.

"O'Doud," Osgood said, "quick as I find Mrs. Gilpatrick and rescue her from those two yahoos who kidnapped her, I'll be back. You might want to make arrangements for your daughter before then, because you'll be away for a quite a while."

Selah, stubbornly, had remained within earshot. Her skirt rustled as she whirled. "Daddy? What does he mean, 'you'll be away'?"

"Nothing," O'Doud said coolly. "Mr. Osgood is laying track going the wrong way is all."

Osgood smiled. "It's not my track that went wrong. Let's go, Benny." He stepped to the doorway, gathering in his young deputy and excusing them to Selah, who was watching her father with wide blue eyes.

"Daddy! No!"

The urgency of her cry warned him. Osgood shoved Benny to the side and spun, simultaneously dropping to one knee. He felt the heated passage of a bullet as it caromed over his head.

Black Crossing

Chapter 14

IN THE BACKGROUND of his mind, Osgood heard Selah O'Doud make an odd, mewling sound. In front of him, Colin O'Doud was thumbing the hammer of a long-barreled Colt for a second shot. He wouldn't miss a second time.

Lunging to the right, Osgood swept his .44 from the holster. His forefinger squeezed the trigger as he brought the pistol to bear, certain that, without taking time to aim, the shot would miss. His ears roared with the thunder of gunfire in the closed space. The smell of burned powder stung in his nostrils.

He saw O'Doud hesitate, his eyes grow wide—almost crazed looking—before the man focused again and took deliberate aim at Osgood. But Osgood was collected now, no longer surprised. Calm overtook him. He braced himself and drew a bead on O'Doud's chest. Smooth, deliberate, accurate. He'd been here before. His .44 spoke before the mayor had a chance to squeeze the Colt's trigger.

A brilliant red flower blossomed on the mayor's immaculate white shirtfront.

O'Doud glanced down at himself, his mouth sagging open as though in disbelief. "Selah," he said, his legs collapsing beneath him as he sank to the floor like his bones had melted. A rush of coppery bright blood spurted from the hole in his chest. His pistol, the trigger guard crushed between his finger and the floor, fired reflexively.

Dimly, a startled yelp reached Osgood. Benny. Was he hit? Osgood fired one more time, anxious to end the matter, and prevent O'Doud from shooting again.

O'Doud twisted sideways, falling half behind the big, ornate desk. The Colt jolted from his hand, bouncing beneath the wheels of his desk chair.

The sudden, muffled silence wrapped Osgood in a kind of shock as he shoved his pistol back into the holster. He took a deep breath, coughing as the acrid bite of gunpowder entered his lungs.

"Tompko," he said, turning to search out his deputy, "you all right?"

Benny was kneeling on the floor, Selah O'Doud clasped in his arms. The young deputy's face was pale and distressed. "He shot her, Marshal," he said. "O'Doud shot his own daughter."

Osgood forced words through the obstruction in his throat. "Is she dead?"

Tompko shook his head. "No, sir. I don't believe she's hurt too bad. I think she fainted."

Forcing his dulled mind to think, Osgood stepped forward. "Where's she hit?"

"Grazed her ribs," Benny said. "Spun her around like a top."

Osgood nodded. "I'll get the hostler. He can ride into town and fetch the doc. Ritter, too. We're going to need the undertaker. Meanwhile, I'm going after Ione."

Benny stared at him with his mouth open. "And leave this girl alone? We can't do that."

"We're not going to. You'll stay here with her—and him." Osgood jerked his head toward O'Doud's body before taking out his Smith & Wesson and filling the empty chambers with cartridges. He still felt shaky—the aftermath of killing a man. Of being shot at himself. Slowly, he walked over to the cabinet where he'd once seen O'Doud locate the bottle of Irish whiskey. He found the whiskey, pulled the cork with his teeth and tilted the bottle to his mouth. Swallowed once, deeply. The liquor burned his gullet, clearing away the dregs of gunpowder and the miasma from his brain.

A little to his own surprise, he discovered the one drink was all he wanted. Setting the bottle down, he walked toward the front of the house where the door stood open.

The old man was hunkered on the porch just outside. He appeared to be waiting for the marshal to notice him.

"I seen you," the hostler said. "I seen you shoot him. But I seen him shoot first. Seen him hit Miss Selah." He spat a stream of dark brown tobacco juice over the edge of the porch. "Good riddance he's gone, I say. A man oughtn't to shoot his own daughter."

Osgood couldn't disagree. "He was trying for me," he said.

"I know it. He oughtn't to have missed." Art spat again. "He was gonna shoot you in the back, mister. And him the mayor. Don't seem right for a man set up like him."

"Not right for anyone," Osgood said. "I want you to ride into town, old-timer. We need help out here. You feel up to it?"

Art creaked upward onto his feet. "I heard you telling the deputy. Bring Doc Worthy, bring Ritter. That boy going to take care of Miss Selah?"

"That boy" protested at length at being left behind to play mammy to Selah O'Doud. Tompko was seeing him off from the porch, where he could hear if Selah woke up. Osgood overrode his objections.

"We don't have time to wait, Benny," he said, climbing onto his gelding. He smoothed the animal's neck. "This horse better be able to run because they've got a two hour start on me. The road's powerful rough, too. I just hope Ione—"

"Ride over to Harrison and catch the steamer," Benny advised. "That's shorter. The General Sherman should be docking about the time you get there. They make the trip a deal faster than a man on horseback. It'll take you right to the train depot in Coeur d'Alene City."

It was a good idea, one Osgood, in his concern for Ione, hadn't thought of. He lifted his hand to Benny. "You're a good man, Benny, and a fine deputy."

Tompko's face flushed with pleasure. "Go, Mr. Osgood. Don't let those yahoos hurt Miz Gilpatrick."

Osgood set spurs to the brown gelding, loping along the track that was becoming familiar to them both. A bit later they turned off onto the road to Harrison and Osgood asked the horse to run. He did.

***

HARRISON LANDING WAS a town much like Black Crossing, in that it was built primarily for and depended on the timber industry. In the last few years, it had become a stop on the way up the Coeur d'Alene River as the steamboats carried men and supplies to the silver mines in the mountains. Made up of a few saloons, a store, a sawmill and a few houses, the town sprawled along the banks of the river, spilling over to the lakeshore. Wooden docks jutted into both the river and the lake. Log pilings stuck out of the water, their edges as uneven as broken gray teeth.

To a man accustomed to the sheer volume of men, ships and commerce along San Francisco Bay, Harrison was small potatoes, but Osgood greeted the sight of the lake steamer, General Sherman, with relief. The boat was just bringing up its boilers, ready to haul a load of ore and men over to Coeur d'Alene City. Osgood paid the fare for himself and his horse, easing the nervous animal up a hollow-sounding gangplank, only to have him try to bolt with the steamer's first whistle.

It was cold on the water, Osgood discovered, once they were under way. Standing outside the boat's cabin, he shivered in his lightweight coat. If he lived through the next few hours, he'd have Bessinger order in a heavy jacket for him and some mud boots. Maybe double the order so Tompko wasn't forever stinking up the office with his wet socks.

The weak sun was losing ground to low clouds and a freshening wind that stirred the lake into a choppy, white-capped froth. The heavily laden boat cut sluggishly through the waves, leaving Osgood free to plot his next move.

If Selah was right, Jensen and the other man—what had she called him? Covich?—would have taken Ione straight to the train. Their ultimate destination might be California, but he'd bet on them taking the first train out of town, no matter which way it was headed. They'd be wise enough to know Osgood would be after them, even with O'Doud trying to put him off the trail. Osgood didn't figure Jensen would put much reliance on his boss flat out killing Osgood in a face off. Meanwhile, they'd try to fool Osgood by boarding a train that ran the wrong way, then switch direction later.

He didn't figure to let things go that far.

Osgood shifted impatiently, his arms resting on the rail. He stood close to his horse, where he could quiet it, in case the creature acted up again. He didn't want it jumping over the rail.

What would Ione be doing? he wondered. Struggling? Crying? Screaming for help? Osgood didn't imagine she would accept being kidnapped without a fight. He purely hurt for her. Was there anyone who would heed her cries if she called out? Or would passersby turn their heads and deafen their ears, afraid to tangle with a man like Jensen, who wore the guise of gunslinger openly, like a badge. Afraid also, of that hulking, dark-faced man Osgood had seen dining with Jensen. He'd looked strong enough to chew up trees and spit out toothpicks.

But Ione was a stubborn lady, with enough starch in her spine to stand up to most anybody. He took heart from that.

During the afternoon, the General Sherman dodged into coves to pick up men or goods. Osgood thought he might have enjoyed the excursion, had he not been in such a hurry. As it was, he claimed priority of official business, and was the first off the gangplank when the steamer tied up at the Coeur d'Alene City wharf. The train depot was no great distance from their loading dock, and knowing the way from when he'd first arrived in the area, he mounted up and headed straight there.

A train was standing at the station, the engine pointed west. Lackadaisical puffs of steam burped from its brass stack, only to be blown into rags against the leaden sky. The engine was at rest for the moment, Osgood noted. He had time to go at this slowly and cautiously, to think of a way to lessen Ione's danger. If this was even the right train.

For the most part, the train was made up of open cars filled with ore. More of them waited on the wharf and were in the process of being loaded with the ore bags trundled off the General Sherman. When filled, they'd be attached at the end of the train. Baggage was being loaded into a closed boxcar, along with a sack of what looked like mail, and some ironbound chests. Two passenger cars were hitched on behind the baggage. After that was a cattle car, empty except for three horses. One of them was Ione's mare.

Osgood's heart thudded. He was in time. They hadn't yet left.

***

SHE HAD FOUGHT—and lost. Ione knew that much, although the battle had already paled in her memory. Become far away and unreal. She also knew she was on a horse, enduring a nightmare ride on a trail to nowhere—unless that was not real either. She saw trees rushing out of the night straight at her, looming sentinels warning of doom. They bore hanged men in their branches, dangling from limbs like heavy fruit. The hanged men all wore Isaac's face. She ducked beneath the onslaught, crying out in terror, in grief.

Only then the trees became mere trees again, soon left behind, replaced by more just like them. Over and over.

The men with her—those evil men—laughed at first, until Jensen grew tired of her cries.

"Christ, Covich, what's the matter with her? She going crazy?"

"Gave her a little too much. It'll wear off quick enough."

"Christ!" And then, since he couldn't cuff his partner, Jensen hit her instead.

Ione believed her visions were illusions. Isaac wasn't really hanging in those trees. She knew Marshal Osgood had taken him down, given him a decent burial. Her son rested safe, and she had attended his funeral.

So that made these horrible visions a symptom of the drug Covich had crammed between her teeth as Jensen forced open her mouth. Within moments, the opium had taken hold. Her mind became bedlam, time a blur, vision an inflated balloon. Somewhere along the way, she was aware another man had joined them. His hated voice rose above the others, and she wept.

But she could not sustain her wailing for long, and when it died away, it was almost as if she were unconscious, an automaton, doing exactly what Jensen told her to do, even though it wasn't what she wanted. If she defied him, the rebellion earned her another slap. She hardly felt them, if he only knew. It was the weakness she hated, and him. Her hate made her stronger. She felt it coursing through her veins, battling the opium for supremacy.

Presently, they arrived at a familiar barn, where she dismounted when told, realizing as she did so that she'd been riding astride her sidesaddle. Her legs were sore where they'd been rubbed raw.

A bewhiskered old man, also familiar, led Nellie away. Nellie. Her only friend. Jensen took her arm in a rough hold and dragged her higgledy-piggledy up a path, then into a house where they all ended up in Colin O'Doud's office.

Selah's voice came to her. "What's the matter with Ione? Is she sick?"

A rumbled reply, then Selah again, "Make her give it back, Daddy. It's mine."

The door closed behind them, shutting Selah out, shutting her in with her son's murderers.

She had vowed vengeance, she remembered, feeling herself sway where she stood, but now the drug silenced her and left her unable to help herself.

"Sit her down before she falls down," O'Doud said, and when the edge of the chair touched the backs of her legs, she dropped onto it as though she had no bones beneath her skin.

The mayor questioned her, his voice coming from far away, asking what she knew, what Osgood knew, who they'd told, what they planned.

She said nothing, locked in her silence, her head drooping on her neck. Once he grasped her chin in his fingers and made her look up at him, demanding she answer him. It made her dizzy and she retched, whereupon he cursed and jumped away.

"Puke on my floor and I'm make you eat it off the rug like a dog."

And like a dog—a mad dog—she would attack him, she thought, and set her teeth to his throat.

But after an endless time he gave up the relentless inquisition and said to Jensen, "What the hell. She doesn't know anything. Take her away. Dispose of her however you want."

"However we want?" That was Covich.

She tried to curse him, but the words wouldn't come out.

"What about Osgood?" Jensen asked in a mumble.

"I'll take care of Osgood," the mayor replied.

In a dim way, Ione realized this must mean TJ was alive, although she'd been afraid he was already dead.

Then it was back out to the barn, Jensen and Covich dragging her between them like a sack of feed. They tied her on Nellie, and they rode. They rode and rode and the trees alongside the trail rushed at her wearing the decomposing face of her son. She was soundless in her shock and horror.

***

THE MAN behind the ticket counter in the depot was eager enough to talk, once he got a glimpse of Osgood's badge.

"You're from Black Crossing, eh? I heard there was some trouble there a while back. Heard the marshal was murdered. Guess that wasn't you."

"Guess not." Osgood, forcing a grin, pushed his impatience aside. Appreciate a man's wit, and his memory was apt to improve as well. "Though not for lack of trying. I'm in Coeur d'Alene City looking for a couple of men who abducted a woman out of Black Crossing. I've got reason to believe they may be taking this train."

"This train?" The ticket agent looked honestly appalled that hooligans could be using his train for their reprehensible schemes. "What do they look like, Marshal? Maybe I'll remember them."

Osgood's description of Jensen and Covich was succinct; of Ione, it was more eloquent.

"Why, that sounds like the doctor fella who's escorting a poor sick woman and her brother over to the coast. He said she'd die if she didn't get treated at a sanatorium that specializes in her sort of ailment. I don't know what it is. But, Marshal, I've got to tell you, she looked pretty bad, all pale and wan. Kind of swoony like. The doctor was keeping her on her feet, while the brother bought their tickets. They said it wasn't catching," he added, as though to reassure himself.

"On her feet?" What did the man mean? Was she hurt? Terrorized, perhaps, into submission? Not that Ione would be easy to terrorize. He knew she was a fighter.

"Yeah." The ticket agent squinted his eyes behind tiny, wire-rimmed spectacles in an effort to remember. "He had his arm around her, see, like he thought she might be going to faint."

Or make a break, Osgood added to himself.

"She's just a little bit of a woman. Got dark hair. That sound like the woman you're searching for?" At Osgood's nod, he added, "She looked kind of strange, now I think of it. Her eyes."

"Eyes?"

"Yeah. Big around as a double eagle, they were. And her face—drawn and white."

Osgood hoped the man was inventing as he went along, caught up in the drama of the moment. Her eyes, though. Sounded to him like they might have dosed her with opium. The only good thing about the situation he could see was in them going to that much trouble. If they were intent on keeping her quiet, they must not mean to kill her. They'd already had plenty of chances for that on the way here, and there had been plenty of hiding spots for a body, too.

But there were other kinds of harm, his inner voice reminded him. Aloud, he said, "Thanks. Did you see which car they boarded?"

The ticket agent's help ended here. "Sorry. Can't say. I wasn't watching. Hope you find them, Marshal." He looked over the top of Osgood's head. "Next."

Osgood headed for the passenger cars, coming up on them from the rear in an effort to stay out of sight of the windows. The trouble here, he knew, was that Jensen could easily spot him first. If Covich hadn't been paying attention last night at dinner, he probably wouldn't know Osgood right off, but even Ione might give him away if she was drugged and not thinking clearly.

Finding the conductor standing on the second car's rear platform having a smoke was an unexpected piece of luck. Osgood flashed his badge.

"Lead car." The conductor answered Osgood's question without hesitation. "I noticed in particular. Two well-dressed men, with coats and a valise each. The woman ain't got but a sweater on and her dress is torn. No luggage."

Ione had been wearing a sweater when they went to check the log decks, Osgood remembered. It had been warm yesterday, for the end of October. Today it was colder.

"How many other people are in the car?"

The conductor shrugged. "A few. It's filling up fast. The folks you're talking about took a seat at the back."

Which wouldn't necessarily make Ione's rescue any easier. Jensen and Covich were bound to be alert, watching every passenger who boarded the train. Seemed to him there was only one way to handle the situation, and that was to move fast and steady.

"Maybe you could stop anyone else from boarding," he suggested. "Fewer people in the line of fire, the better. Better send for the sheriff, too."

The conductor's face drew tight. "I'll do it. Is there going to be shooting, Marshal?"

"I hope not." But there'd be trouble, all right. He felt the certainty of it in his bones. Flexing his fingers, he removed his coat, loosed the thong over the .44, and stuck his pocket pistol in the waistband of his trousers. He was as ready as he'd ever be. He reminded himself that sometimes it didn't pay to think too much. Fear was apt to put a stranglehold on a man's actions.

The conductor had said the objects of his search were in the farthest car, but Osgood kept a close watch as he passed through the first in line. The top of the head being his first sight of the passengers settled in their high-backed seats, he scanned quickly for the distinctively creased crown of Jensen's hat, or the sheen of dark hair coiled on a woman's neck. He didn't find either. Ione wasn't there. Only a blonde woman with one of those flat Frenchie hats on top, and an elderly female with snow-white locks.

At the forward end, Osgood opened the door a crack before stepping out on the platform between cars. Who knew but what Jensen or the feller passing himself off as a physician would be there. As it happened, he did find two men arguing politics in an amiable manner, but neither was his prey.

He pushed between them, flashing his badge again and hoping his lack of authority in Coeur d'Alene City escaped their notice.

"Get inside the other car," he ordered brusquely. "Take cover. There's apt to be shooting here any minute."

They gaped at him before scrambling away, thankfully silent in their haste. Osgood waited until they were inside with the door shut and then took a deep breath, filling his lungs with air fresh off the lake. It held the scent of evergreen trees, of water, of smoke carried on the wind. Maybe his last good breath. Jensen was a gunslinger by profession, and bound to be faster on the draw than he. A few years younger, too, if no more ruthless, no more determined. Meanwhile, the big man with Jensen was a question mark.

Osgood drew his pistol and reached for the door latch, only to feel it give beneath his hand. The door opened, slamming into him, and nearly tumbling him off the platform. The entry filled with a man and a woman, laughing uproariously at something. The man fell against Osgood and said, "Oh, pardon me," a second before he saw the pistol and staggered backward into the car, pulling the woman with him.

She, too, saw the pistol, and in it, a threat. Her scream, sharp and piercing as the train's whistle, sounded an alarm before Osgood could hush her. Inside the car, the waiting passengers lurched to their feet in unison, turning to stare at the cause of the ruckus. Him. With the rest, not a dozen feet away, was Jensen. And seated beside him, Ione. She looked up at Osgood, her wide dark eyes dazed and vague.

Jensen's pale stare met his. In his hand, trained on Osgood's middle, was one of his twin pistols. His other hand was occupied in controlling Ione. "Well," he said. "If it isn't Marshal TJ Osgood. Can't say as I was expecting you this soon, Marshal."

"You're under arrest, Jensen," Osgood said, "for the abduction of Mrs. Ione Gilpatrick, for the theft of timber belonging to Mr. Jacob Finley, and for attempted murder."

Jensen smiled. "Under arrest? You don't want to do that, Osgood. You're forgetting something. You're forgetting I've got the woman. And you..." His expression changed. "You've got Covich."

More accurately, Covich had Osgood. A pair of arms with muscles thick as ship's hawsers grasped Osgood around the middle and lifted him clear of the floor, all the time squeezing like one of those boa constrictor snakes. His gun hand was trapped between his own body and Covich's. Held almost immobile, within seconds, his fingers began to go numb, the weight of the pistol nearly insupportable. His chest felt as if it were about to cave in.

"TJ," Ione called out, her voice faint. She was trying to stand up, while Jensen kept pushing her down.

"Give it up, Jensen," Osgood panted. "O'Doud is dead." He hadn't much purchase with which to break from Covich's hold, but it didn't stop him from lashing out with his spurred heels and twisting from his shoulders. Neither did much good, except Covich was too busy just hanging on to him to give an all-out try at breaking his back.

At least his head was anchored on securely, Osgood thought, as the bigger man shook him like a terrier shakes a rat. He could think of only one thing to do. Since Covich had him lifted up in such a convenient manner, Osgood flung his head backward with a motion fit to snap his own neck. The tough, sharp brim of his Stetson caught Covich square across the eyes.

The big man howled, let Osgood drop, and threw his hands over his face.

The marshal's feet hit the floor. Whirling, he flipped the .44 up into his fist, slamming the barrel across Covich's face. Blood gushed from a cut across the man's cheekbone and he staggered backward, legs unsteady under the onslaught. Encouraged, Osgood followed, striking him with two more quick taps to the temple until Covich fell, sprawling unconscious onto the dingy floor. Unintentionally, Osgood sprawled along with him, drawn to the ground as the big man sprawled against him.

But it was a lucky thing for Osgood that Covich did drag him down. As his partner collapsed beneath Osgood's attack, Jensen fired. The bullet barely missed Covich as Osgood dove behind the little pot-bellied stove that warmed this end of the railway car. A second bullet pinged against the cast iron, ricocheting into the wood paneling. Jensen ducked behind the seat where Ione sat and disappeared from Osgood's sight.

As though from far away, Osgood became aware of the train passengers. Men were yelling, the women screaming, all diving for cover. They seemed uncertain as to whether they should be supporting Jensen or Osgood, and most of them settled for doing nothing. A few had the presence of mind to escape through the door at the other end of the car, jostling each other unmercifully as they pushed through the exit.

"Hold your fire, Jensen," he shouted over the noise. "Your boss is dead. The war is over."

"Dead?" Jensen yelled back. "How do I know you're not lying?"

"I'm the marshal. I never lie." Or hardly ever. He was lying now. The war wasn't over. Not as long as Jensen held Ione Gilpatrick pinned at his side.

The problem was, Jensen held all the advantage. Osgood was afraid to shoot, because with lead flying every which way, it was hard telling who'd get in the way. And that wasn't all. While Jensen hid behind the train seat and Ione Gilpatrick's skirts, Osgood had, for cover, a pot-bellied stove hot enough to burn the whiskers off his face.

At his left, the human mountain he'd just pistol-whipped— a prescription that would kill most men—groaned and tried to sit up.

"Give up, Jensen," Osgood said again.

Jensen peered between seats—a brief glimpse—too quick to provide Osgood with a clear shot. "You said the boss is dead. How do you know?"

Osgood hesitated. It was a loaded question. "Because I'm the one killed him," he said finally.

Jensen grunted. "A shootout? Man to man and face to face?"

"Near enough." Osgood scooted to the opposite side of the stove, the better to singe the other side of his face for a while.

"Well, now," Jensen said slowly. "So you beat him. But I wonder if you can beat me, Marshal. What do you say we see? Winner takes the woman."

Beside him, Ione twisted free long enough to cry, "No. TJ. Don't do it."

"Shut up," Jensen snarled.

Osgood heard a smack and Ione's stifled gasp. Rage searing through his veins, he jockeyed around the stove again, shuffling for a better view. The gunslinger, he discovered, was backing up the isle towards the other end of the car, dragging Ione with him and using her for a shield. She caught at the seats as they went, hanging on to each one until Jensen jerked her free. With every yank at her arm, he seemed to grow angrier.

"Ione, be careful," Osgood called.

But she was helping. Jensen's pistol wavered as he paused yet again to draw her with him. They were only a few feet from the exit when she gave Osgood his chance. Jensen had grown to expect her resistance. He was caught unprepared when she snapped out of her drug-induced stupor and sprang at him, butting her head into his chest.

Staggered by her ferocity, Jensen tripped, catching himself with the hand he'd been using to hold her. Quick and lithe as a doe, Ione jumped away and darted between seats, trapped for certain if Osgood couldn't protect her.

The marshal lunged to his feet, staggering forward with his bad leg barely holding under the punishment. "Jensen!" he roared.

A fraction of a second later he realized he should've saved his breath. Just shot the son of a bitch. Fire burned across his wrist as Jensen's bullet grazed past. He managed to hang onto the pistol, but suddenly nerveless fingers refused to obey commands to pull the trigger. For precious seconds, Jensen had the advantage. Right up until Ione darted out into plain sight and screamed something unintelligible—maybe her son's name. She was pointing Jensen's other pistol, snaked from his holster during their collision, and was pointing it straight at his chest, the barrel remarkably steady.

Undecided, Jensen made a quick move towards Ione, changed his mind, and whirled to face Osgood.

"This is it, Osgood," he said. There was a sheen of sweat on his forehead. "Time to find out who's the fastest."

Did Jensen think he was stupid enough to fall into that trap? Osgood wondered. Did he expect Osgood to try and out-duel him? Blood cascaded down his wrist and dripped from his fingers, the pistol grip slick with it. No contest.

"Put your gun down, Jensen, and step away from Mrs. Gilpatrick." Osgood's .44 swung loose at his side. He hadn't the power to raise it.

"You shoot, I shoot," Ione said.

Jensen's pale eyes flicked toward her once, dismissed her, and found Osgood again. They narrowed, centered, and bored into Osgood. He blinked, jerked his pistol in an arc, and fired on the upward motion. The bullet plowed into the floor of the railroad car a scant two feet in front of the marshal. A splinter stabbed into Osgood's boot.

There wasn't a thing Osgood could do, but then, he didn't have to. Ione kept her word. She fired and kept on firing, until six bullet holes, six bright splashes of blood, six small couriers of death formed a round pattern on the front of Jensen's gray shirt. He stood a moment in the echoing noise, a look of shocked disbelief on his thin face, then he fell over.

Jensen had not been nearly as good a gunslinger as he'd thought. Osgood almost laughed, but without taking his eyes from Jensen, until he was certain the gunman wouldn't be getting up. Then he walked over and kicked the Colt from

Jensen's fingers. The railroad car stank of blood and burned powder. Some of the blood was his own.

"Are you hit?" he asked Ione.

Ione's barely audible whisper came to him, soft after the crack of gunfire in the enclosed Pullman car. "I'm all right. He's dead, isn't he?" Like wind escaping a sail, she sank onto the nearest seat.

He knelt beside the fallen man, setting his forefinger on Jensen's neck. "As a mackerel."

A deep, trembling sigh racked through her. "Good."

Osgood limped over to where she sat and leaned down, taking the pistol from her hand and lifting her up. Her legs were still unsteady, the pupils of her eyes huge in the greeny-brown irises. It was amazing she'd been able to help herself, he thought, proud of her pluck. More amazing that she'd been able to help him.

"Did either of them hurt you?" His simple words asked more than they seemed.

She shook her head. Then, squinting over his shoulder, cried, "TJ! Look out."

Whirling, Osgood found the strength to thumb the hammer back on his pistol. Covich, in the act of drawing his weapon from an underarm holster, thought better of the action and raised his arms in surrender.

"Guess you've got me," he said, grinning wryly, with a show of crooked teeth.

"Don't you make a move, Covich," Osgood ordered. "It'd be a pleasure to lay you out alongside Jensen. Ione, there's a set of handcuffs in my back pocket. Get them and cuff Covich. Don't worry. I won't let him touch you. Just don't step in front of my gun." He paused. "You're not scared, are you?"

For the first time in their acquaintance, he saw Ione Gilpatrick smile. Her slim hand moved slowly and steadily to his pocket and withdrew the cuffs. "Not anymore, TJ."

Chapter 15

IF IT HADN'T BEEN for Ione, Osgood had a notion he might've been taking up space in the Coeur d'Alene City jail alongside Covich. Instead, he was seated across the desk from Sheriff Farnsworth in a position of honor, with Ione on the chair next to him. Still, it was easy to see Farnsworth didn't appreciate a stranger coming into his town and causing a uproar.

"Your reputation precedes you, Osgood," he said. "My jail is already filled with the miscreants you've sent here from Black Crossing. Now the county has to deal with 'em." He didn't appear any too happy about the arrangement.

Osgood thought maybe, judging by his sour expression, the county sheriff had already received a complaint from the manager of the Northern Pacific Railroad Line. The passengers chased from their seats in fear of their lives had been a vocal lot. And then there was Jensen's blood staining the seats and floor. Some of his own, too. Osgood sighed, too tired, his wrist hurting too much, to care.

Although Ione looked like she'd been dragged through a knothole, what with her skirt mussed with horse hair and sweat, and her sweater torn and unraveling at the elbow, there was no doubting she was a lady. Consequently, Farnsworth deigned to listen to her story before he threw away the key on Osgood.

"If Mr. Osgood hadn't come to fetch me before the train left," she said, shivering a little and pulling the sweater more tightly around her, "I'd have been sold into slavery like in the days before the late war."

"Now wait a min—" Farnsworth started, but Ione cut him off.

"White slavery," she overrode his protest, making Jensen's intentions toward her clear.

"Ma'am," said Farnsworth, "you can't know that."

"Can't I? But he told me so himself."

"He was probably just trying to scare you, or keep you quiet."

"He had drugs for that. And he knew I was plenty scared already. Are you defending him?" Ione's eyes were still dilated from the opium Jensen had forced down her throat. Bruises on the fine skin of her neck and jaw showed fingerprints where one of the men had opened her mouth when she wouldn't do so herself.

"No, ma'am," Farnsworth muttered, "I'm not defending him. But it is hard to believe a man like Colin O'Doud hired these thugs to do the things you folks say he did."

From his pocket, Osgood drew out the lengthy message a boy from the telegraph office had brought to him while he and Ione had been waiting for Farnsworth. He'd had time to read it several times over.

"This might explain things," he said, passing it to the Coeur d'Alene City sheriff.

Farnsworth took the flimsy like he suspected it had teeth. "What does it say?"

"When my deputy was here the day before yesterday," Osgood replied, "I had him send down to San Francisco for information on O'Doud. This is the reply. Feller from the telegraph office brought it to me when he heard I was here." It hadn't taken long for news of the shooting to spread through town, or to make known who was in the midst of it.

Farnsworth studied the signature. "This person reliable?"

"Pinkerton Agent-in-charge of the San Francisco office," Osgood said. The answer seemed to satisfy the sheriff, who perched a pair of spectacles on his nose and slowly read through the lengthy missive. Osgood figured he'd be getting the bill for the information, one of these fine days. Nothing was free.

The telegram read:

PETER JENSEN—Stop—Served four years in San Quentin 1882 to 1886—Stop—Paroled to Colin O'Doud—Stop—Colin O'Doud—Stop—No prison record—Stop—Arrested assault of wife's father—Stop—Charge dropped—Stop—O'Doud arrested embezzlement of funds—Stop—No conviction—Stop—Money not recovered—Stop—Started investment consortium—Stop—No investments recorded—Stop—Other investors sued to recover money—Stop—Money not recovered—Stop

FARNSWORTH GLANCED at Osgood over the tops of his specs. "Well," he said, a little grudgingly, "looks like we know how O'Doud got his start. And why he came to Idaho Territory. Says here he's got more debts than an honest man could pay if he lived two lifetimes."

"And explains why he was willing to kill," Osgood said. "O'Doud was a man who liked his ease and his position. Building that fancy house of his in the middle of the backwoods never made any sense to me."

"Home away from home." Farnsworth snorted. "Reckon he couldn't show his face back in California."

"Yes." Ione's hands clenched on her skirt, bunching the fabric into a knot. Her voice sounded quite calm. "Isaac told me Marshal Blodgett got a telegram from San Francisco the day he was murdered. O'Doud must've heard about it, assumed his game was up, and had Jensen kill the marshal before the news got around. It was my son's misfortune to be on hand, afraid to tell anyone about what he'd seen. O'Doud used his daughter to prevent Isaac from speaking out, and when he wavered, had him killed. I told you," she insisted, speaking to Osgood.

"Yes, you did. And found the proof, too." Without thinking, Osgood fished a comparatively clean handkerchief from his vest pocket and mopped at the tears sliding down Ione's face. She hardly seemed aware of them. When he was finished, she took his hand, his good hand, gripping it tightly.

Farnsworth cleared his throat. "But you, Osgood. He went to California and hired you."

A flush climbed from Osgood's neck into his face. He flicked Ione a glance before releasing her. Ione Gilpatrick was hanging on his words, and he hesitated, dreading laying himself open to her contempt. He doubted she'd want to be anywhere near him when she found out what he'd been before.

"Sneaked in. I suppose he thought bringing me here was worth the chance of being seen," he said at last.

Farnsworth leaned forward. "And why would that be, Osgood?"

Osgood stood up, settling his Stetson on his head. He avoided looking at Ione's face. "My name was splashed around a good bit in the tabloids at one time, Farnsworth. Made myself something of an unsavory reputation. It happened round about the same time O'Doud was answering questions regarding his honesty. I assume in reading about himself, he read about me. I expect he recognized my name when I applied, and figured I needed the work bad enough I'd do anything to get it."

"But you wouldn't," Ione said.

"No."

"Why was your name in the papers?" Farnsworth asked.

Osgood shook his head.

"If you'n me are going to be neighbors," the sheriff said, "I want to know what kind of man I'm dealing with. Can I trust you, or not?"

Would they be working together? Osgood wondered. Or would the story go around until he felt shamed into moving on again, forever looking for a place to put down roots?

Ione Gilpatrick stood up, too, as if she thought she was leaving with him. "You can trust him," she told Farnsworth.

Her confidence warmed him, although he doubted it would still be there when she knew what he'd done. Best to tell his story himself. "I used to drink," he admitted. "Too much. I made some stupid mistakes when under the influence. Then I made one that got a good man killed. Got me fired."

"But you don't drink now." Surprising him, Ione touched his arm. "I know. I watched that night at O'Doud's. And I saw how he reacted. Now I know why he tried to kill you, just like he did Marshal Blodgett. He discovered he couldn't buy your loyalty."

She knew! Osgood's heartbeat thudded in thanksgiving. In release.

One of the Coeur d'Alene City deputies interrupted, coming in and mumbling into Farnsworth's ear. The sheriff planted his palms on the desk and grunting, pushed himself to his feet. "Well, folks," he said, his ire with Osgood apparently forgotten, "I won't say it's been a pleasure, but I'm glad to have this blight on the territory removed. I'll be seeing you again, no doubt, when all these gents you've saddled me with come to trial."

He and Osgood shook hands, and he nodded to Ione. "Ma'am, my condolences on losing your son."

***

SOMEONE HAD TAKEN the horses off the train and over to the livery, picking up Osgood's brown gelding along the way.

He figured he'd part with Ione here, on the boardwalk outside the sheriff's office, find his horse and leave. Alone.

He didn't imagine there was any reason for Ione to return to Black Crossing now her son was cleared, the instigators of his death either dead or in custody. Anyway, Jensen had destroyed most of her things. She'd need to buy everything new, provided she had any money, and if not, he could spare some. Leonard could wait a while for him to buy the horse.

No. There was nothing to hold her in the town that had made lynching her boy easy.

With these thoughts running through his mind, Osgood was considerably surprised when Ione tucked her hand into the crook of his arm and started off with him toward the livery. Of course, he reminded himself. She'd want to sell her pony. Though a poor specimen, it would bring a few dollars.

Trying to ignore the sense of loss already making him morose, thinking of her need, Osgood said, "Why'd Jensen tear through your cabin the way he did? Looked to me like nothing is left." He couldn't stop himself from turning the knife in the wound. His wound or hers.

He glanced past the livery, just so he wouldn't have to watch her reaction. Out on the lake, the green water looked thick and cold. Inside himself, he felt as bleak as the scene.

Her free hand touched just above her heart. "He was looking for something. Something he thought I'd taken from the O'Doud house. But when he followed me home, it was to Isaac's house, and he discovered I was not Mrs. Fane, but Mrs. Gilpatrick. I thought he was going to kill me then, but Covich stopped him." She paused. "He had a better idea of what to do with me."

Something about the explanation reminded Osgood of O'Doud's accusation and stirred his curiosity. "Did you?" His question seemed incredulous even as he asked it. "Take something, I mean?"

But although pink dots colored her cheeks, she nodded. "Yes. I certainly did. A locket Isaac had given Selah. It belonged to my mother, and it contained a miniature painting of Isaac as a child. It meant nothing to her, thrown down on her dressing table with two others and dusted with rice powder. But it meant everything to me."

"You have it safe?"

She touched her heart again. "Yes."

They had reached the door of the livery. Through the dim opening, Osgood could see his horse standing patiently, swishing his tail at a few flies the nippy fall weather had made lethargic. Ione's piebald pony was next to the brown in the same stall. They seemed almost companionable.

"Are you going to stay in Black Crossing, TJ?" she asked, tugging at his arm to stop him before they entered.

The question surprised him, although not as much as her comfortable use of his name. "Thomas Jefferson," he said. He wanted to kiss her goodbye, he discovered. It had been long time since he kissed a woman—a good woman.

"Pardon me?"

"TJ. It stands for Thomas Jefferson. But nobody ever called me by it."

He saw she was biting back a smile.

"TJ, are you?"

He'd almost forgotten what she asked. "I reckon. Unless the council fires me for shooting the mayor."

At this, she turned and started into the barn. "They won't. You're too good a lawman. I'll be staying, too. Maybe the town will need a schoolteacher. I can't leave Isaac there by himself," she added at his questioning frown.

He had the sudden sensation of that lump in his chest melting. She wasn't leaving. He'd see her again.

"The thing is..." She hesitated, then plunged on. "My cabin is ruined. I don't have anywhere to live."

Osgood felt like laughing. Even his wounded wrist didn't seem to hurt anymore. "I'll help you," he said. "The whole town'll turn out to help you."

But he would be first in line. And then they'd see what happened.

THE END

About the Author

C.K. Crigger was born and raised in North Idaho on the Coeur d'Alene Indian Reservation, and currently lives with her husband, three feisty little dogs and an uppity Persian cat in Spokane Valley, Washington.

Imbued with an abiding love of western traditions and wide-open spaces, Crigger writes of free-spirited people who break from their standard roles.

Her short story, Aldy Neal's Ghost, was a 2007 Spur finalist. Black Crossing, won the 2008 EPIC Award in the historical/western category. Letter of the Law was a 2009 Spur finalist in the audio category.

Find more great titles by C.K. Crigger and Wolfpack Publishing at:

http://wolfpackpublishing.com/c-k-crigger/

49315324R00119

Made in the USA
Middletown, DE
13 October 2017